Shakespeare's Diaries

by

Steven Cutts

Published by New Generation Publishing in 2018

Copyright © Steven Cutts 2018

First Edition

The author asserts the moral right under the Copyright, Designs and Patents Act 1988 to be identified as the author of this work.

All Rights reserved. No part of this publication may be reproduced, stored in a retrieval system or transmitted, in any form or by any means without the prior consent of the author, nor be otherwise circulated in any form of binding or cover other than that which it is published and without a similar condition being imposed on the subsequent purchaser.

www.newgeneration-publishing.com

Dedication

For Charis Orchard Feeney
For not knowing how to give up

Chapter 1

Let's face it, not all of us know where we're going.

How, for example, had Crispin Shakespeare envisaged his own life turning out on the day he first walked into medical school? Not like this, that's for sure. Back then, Stratford had been his past and medicine had been his future. In Crispin's tiny little mind, there were field hospitals to be worked in and fantastical new drugs to discover. And whatever direction he took, his 18-year-old self had never had any doubts about his ultimate destination: New York, or failing that the less parochial city of London.

That was then. This was now. Ten years down the line, Crispin was driving to work in his all singing, all dancing English sports car. There was dew on the grass, hay in the fields and plenty of fresh air, as he raced along a country lane at a little under thirty.

Sweeping around another corner, Crispin passed a familiar road sign, 'Shakespeare's Birthplace – 2 miles'.

Actually, it was nearly three, but Britain was like that and a few minutes later, Crispin was waiting at the final junction before Stratford. Suddenly, a long white lorry screeched to a halt on his left, blocking his view and forcing him to look up. Pushing his head out of the window, the big man in the lorry eyed up the open topped vehicle from above, shouting, "Do you want to do a straight swap?"

The driver, it seemed, had a weakness for English sports cars although it was hard to imagine how he could ever fit in one.

"Urgent business!" he called, nodding to the container behind him. "I've got Hamlet's skull in here!"

Bored by the driver, Crispin's attention returned to the lorry. The letters RSC had been sprayed in jet black and

1

there was something beautifully retro about the style. It was about as long a vehicle as any he had ever seen and it could – presumably – ship an entire stage production to any theatre in the land.

"They're on tour!" called Crispin, who liked to keep abreast of these things.

The lorry pulled away and Crispin decided to give it a few seconds before moving on. A string of brightly coloured buildings soon followed and a short while later, the street became ordinary. Over to the right, an abandoned pub had been marked for demolition and a man in a JCB was busy performing this task. A score of men in hard hats were standing around it, with a couple of weather beaten skips for the slag. Crispin's Morgan waited for the lights to turn green and then, without warning, one of the builders vanished in a puff of smoke.

There was no sound.

Crispin checked his mirrors. The road was clear and there was nothing behind him. Doing a quick U-turn, he came to a noisy halt on the far pavement and leapt bodily from the vehicle. On the building site, alarm bells were sounding and men in bright yellow hats had gathered around a broad and new found defect in the soil.

It was time to join in. Approaching the edge of the abyss, Crispin saw a layer of exposed top soil and beneath that, a laminate of hardened brick. A little further down, the bricks cut out and a seam of rotting planks began. The builders had stumbled across an ancient cellar and the land above it had literally collapsed beneath their feet.

"Bob!" shouted the man next to Crispin. "Bob? 'Yer alright?"

But there was no response.

"It may be dangerous to move him," said Crispin, sounding very earnest.

Britain is a deeply class divided society and Crispin's calm and measured tones caused a stir amongst the builders.

"What are you then?" came a voice. "Are you a doctor?"

"That's Doctor Shakespeare!" yelled a stout little man in blue. "You're my wife's doctor!" he added, waving with a toothless grin. "She talks about you!"

Crispin lacked the kind of specialist equipment he needed to enter the hole, but he was willing to improvise. He asked for a rope and the builders produced one with remarkable speed. And then he tied one end of the rope to the JCB and threw the rest of it into the sinkhole. The loose, middle part of the rope was soon wrapped around his waist and then he shuffled backwards towards the edge of the hole and felt it take the strain. Would it hold him?

Yes.

"Are you going to go down on your own?" asked another voice. "Someone might miss you at the hospital."

They were throwing in humour at a time where humour was hardly called for, but this is what men do in such situations and Crispin had an answer on standby.

"I'm in General Practice," he told them and stepped back into the abyss.

Most of the dust had already settled and in its upper part, the margins of the defect were plain to see. Crispin saw a layer of chalk like soil and then, suddenly, blackened clay. Harder rock and mud soon followed until finally, and at its lowest level, a wall of neatly laid bricks appeared against his feet. But his descent had been too rapid and the rope had all but burnt through his cords. Crispin spotted something large and solid, jutting out from the side and decided to rest one shoe against it. A few feet up above him, something decided to part company with the wall, skirting his face on its way to the floor.

Staying still was not an option. Shifting his weight to the brick, Crispin worked the rope onto a fresh patch of corduroy and fell some more, until his feet hit the ground and his patient began to moan.

Just like my day job, mused the doctor. *None of them bloody grateful.*

"Who are you then?" came a voice in the darkness. "How'd you get here?"

"I used to climb."

Crispin searched his pockets and quickly produced a pen torch. It was a fresh, state of the art sort of thing that one of the drug reps had given him and a dazzling beam of light soon swept across the scene. As expected, the injured builder was right beside his feet but what struck Crispin hardest was the sheer scale of the room itself. This was much more than an ill-defined air pocket. It was a walled and purposefully built chamber, leading out onto a row of solid steps and ending blindly in a wooden door.

Crispin knelt down and checked the man's pulse. It was fast and furious but it was there.

"I can walk!" groaned the man, who was about to discover that he couldn't. A heavy wooden beam had chased him down the sinkhole and pinned him to the floor. If Crispin wanted to complete his mission, he was going to have to move it.

He tried. He couldn't. He took the strain again, this time with real determination and the beam jolted and rolled into the blackness.

"I could have gotten that off." Called Bob. "I could have gotten that off on my own. If you'd given me more time."

Crispin reached down and tried to help, but the man refused a request to stand up. Meanwhile, things were happening on the surface. Blue flashing lights had joined the JCB and a fresh set of voices were shouting down. Within minutes, they had lowered some kind of harness on a rope, only to discover that Bob was refusing to climb into it. Following a new and lengthy exchange, a fire crew arrived and Bob finally reached the surface in a fluorescent basket.

No doubt the basket would soon return and Crispin would be expected to make the same journey. Conscious that his time in this place might be brief, he decided to explore it in more detail. What function had this chamber once served and why hadn't it appeared on surveyor's charts?

He reached out to a wooden door knob and felt it turn, very slowly in his hand. Seconds later, he entered a second - even more spacious - chamber. Once again, his pen torch blazed into the darkness, but the walls were still distant and the beam seemed to peter out in midair. Closer in, he saw something else: two wooden boxes, abandoned here eons ago by people were were surely long dead. They seemed to sagging very slightly under their own weight and Crispin got the impression that they would be difficult to move.

He ran his fingers across the margins of the first box and sensed only dust. Beneath the covers, both boxes were packed with leather bound books. Lifting one up, Crispin saw a loose sheet of paper and a fading, hand written note.

For a few seconds, he looked back towards the door, concerned that there might be witnesses. Seeing none, he folded the loose sheet of paper and slid it into his pocket. Whilst the significance of the find was far from clear, the instinct to own it was already impossible to resist and for the lost diaries of William Shakespeare, four hundred years of deafening silence were preparing to end.

Chapter 2

A mere 45 minutes later, the only British racing green Morgan in Stratford had arrived at its destination. As a fully paid up partner in the practice, Crispin had been rewarded with his own parking space:

RESERVED FOR DOCTOR CRISPIN SHAKESPEARE

This was it. This was the only realistic solution to his overdraft. His torso was caked in a fine white dust and his tan corduroy trousers were torn beneath the crotch, but that didn't matter. He was here and ready for action.

Secure in his own clinic, Crispin was soon greeted by the shrill tones of the office handset and the practice secretary duly responded.

"Doctor Shakespeare's office?"

The key thing to remember about a telephone call is that the person on the other end can't actually see what you're doing, and today, this was probably a good thing. A few feet to the secretary's left, the eponymous doctor had detached the corrugated plastic tubing from the back of the vacuum cleaner and started to run the thing across his legs. Vacuuming your own clothes whilst actually wearing them was a new and highly effective technique and by the time he was done, Crispin was almost a normal person. A few minutes later, he was busy with an elderly lady and a suspected chest infection. Exploring her sputum pot in depth, Crispin decided to work on the history.

"How long have you had this cough?"

"Oh, a while."

"Well, when did you first notice it?"

"A week tomorrow."

Without sarcasm: "A week tomorrow?" The patient nodded and Crispin gave no comment. Seconds later, his mobile burst into song and he moved to answer.

"Doctor Shakespeare?"

Out of sight and a mile along the road, a woman from the RSC was about to make him an offer.

"Ah, yes, doctor, it's about that room you're trying to let."

RP can sound a bit strange in the West Midlands, but coming from the Royal Shakespeare Company, it wasn't a complete shock.

"I may have just the right person for you." Crispin, who was still high from his abseil, was suddenly elated. "There's a brilliant young American coming to work with us here."

But the lady with the cough was more concerned by his lineage. "You're not the real Shakespeare are you?"

Shielding the microphone with his thumb, Crispin explained that he was not. How the hell had his ancestors managed to saddle him with that title? Years ago, he had seriously considered changing his surname by deed poll, but had never quite had the nerve.

"You're not related?"

"*Nobody's* related," said Crispin, with real conviction. "There was no male line. Look," he muttered, returning to the RSC handset, "he's not going to come back in the middle of the night pretending to be Falstaff, is he?"

"Oh, I shouldn't think so."

"Right then," said Crispin. "See what they offer and let me know if they want to haggle."

The call ended and his secretary reappeared by the door.

"Doctor Shakespeare." She might have been addressing a public meeting. "The senior partner will see you now."

Having settled his affairs with the patient, Crispin decided to give in. The secretary led him along a narrow corridor and gestured to the upcoming door, as if he had never seen it before.

Cutting a very traditional figure in camel trousers and cotton shirt, Crispin's uncle rested heavily in a black leather chair.

"Uncle Jack?" said Crispin, very politely.

"Don't call me Uncle, Crispin! For God's sake! Call me doctor or senior partner or something. Not Uncle. Why don't you just call me Shakespeare?"

"Well, we're all Shakespeares," said the nephew, searching for common ground.

"Ah yes, *Shakespeares*," Jack grumbled. "Just as your father was, God bless him. You missed a real treat there, laddie."

"So I believe."

Concern for the average waiting time had all but disappeared. In its place, came a strange nostalgia for those tiny framed photographs that adorned his office wall. Most children look the same on camera, but the subtle differences in tone and silver can date an image well and the kids in these photographs were both from the 1960s.

"If he hadn't gone to an early grave, he'd be killing himself now, trying to cope with whatever madness you get up to next!" Jack raised one arm and pointed to the window. "What do you call that green thing? Out there in the car park?"

The nephew answered frankly: "It's a car."

"No, young man! It's *money*. Worse than that, it's the bank's money! Now then, your clinic was due to begin at 9 O'clock this morning and it is now clear to me that you did not in fact, *arrive* in that clinic until 10:30. What sort of excuse are you peddling this time?"

"I stopped to attend an injured builder and then, completely by chance, I seem to have stumbled across some sort of mind blowing archaeological find."

The senior partner moved to adjust his pipe. "Doesn't surprise me in the least. And another thing!" he rapped, snatching a new document from his desk: "What's this, here?"

It was an annual leave request, as Crispin was quick to confirm.

"You're not going off to Scotland again with that Thespian crowd?" Something in the nephew's face said that he was. "Your on-going fervour for undergraduate pastimes is driving us all to despair! What about all these debts? How are you going to pay them off?"

Over in their secretary's office, one of the landlines had burst into tune. From Crispin's perspective, this was an opportunity to do a runner, but his Uncle was having none of it.

"...now, the annual practice garden party is due on..."

"September the twenty-second," said Crispin, speaking above the ring tone.

"September the twenty-second." said Jack, as if unprompted. "And this year, it'll be your gig. We're all planning to turn up and we're all expecting the biggest pile of crap in the history of British catering."

By now the practice secretary was back in the office and holding a cordless handset. Sensing a way out, Crispin moved to take it. "Yes? Yes. Two hundred pounds a month? A week! Perfect!" The nephew switched to smiling mode. "Uncle, Jack, Doctor Jack, senior partner in Shakespeare and Co, Stratford Upon Avon. The solution to my financial crisis will be with us this very day." Jack remained skeptical but Crispin wasn't done yet. "I'm taking on a lodger."

"Good God!" barked the uncle. "Are they mad?"

"No!" exclaimed Crispin, defending a tenant he had yet to meet. "Well, they're American."

Chapter 3

To some in the United States, the great universities of the East Coast are an anachronism. Having been founded in the 18th century, they remain a powerful symbol of a shared ancestry and have long surpassed the European centres that spawned them. Princeton, in particular, is a recognised breeding ground for some of the finest minds of their generation and at this very moment, one such mind was about to sit down in the academic common room.

Dumping a pile of papers on the coffee table, Professor Michael Richmond offered this comment to his esteemed colleague.

"Another pile of junk from my sophomore class. I keep thinking one of them might come up with something fresh, but no!"

Across the coffee table, Professor James Smith was showing a distinct lack of interest in Michael's work. Like so many in this room, he had been quietly distracted by the news and unable to think about anything else since he first heard it.

"Sure," said James, with his thoughts still in England. "But can you imagine what will happen if *this thing* is real?" Every Bard expert in the department is going to get it in the neck."

But Professor Richmond took a different view: "James, James!" he started. "This isn't a threat, it's an *opportunity*. Don't you see? Men like us will be able to *clean up* on this new material. There are people out there who think there's nothing left to say about the Bard. Well, there is now. Give it another six weeks and the market for fresh interpretation will be endless."

Richmond had spoken and Smith decided to vanish behind an open copy of the Washington Post.

"Are you planning to dash over yourself?"

"Me? No." said Smith, largely invisible. "But I hear young Arthur got a call."

Thirty yards and a mere nine doors along the corridor, the aforementioned Arthur was sat at his desk and raring to go. Like Professor Richmond, he had spent the last few hours glued to his television and was desperate to hear more.

The door to his office opened and the unshaven academic caught sight of his own name, inscribed as it was in gothic script: *ARTHUR KRANZ PhD*. Kranz was a tenured professor at the University of Princeton, although in some circles, he was better known for a lucrative sideline in antiquities. Some ten years ago, and at the tender age of 33, he had secured the most generous office in this building and today, the place was practically brimming over with memorabilia. Just short of the window, a battered leather suitcase was begging for action. Younger and leaner than most of his peers, Arthur was already speaking to the airlines.

"Yes, I'd like to fly to England, please. Tonight or tomorrow will be fine."

On the other end of the line, a woman did her best to shake his timeline. "I can offer you a ten per cent discount for a weekend flight."

"No!" she heard him snap. "The weekend will be too late."

Turning to face his guest, Kranz pointed to the television screen. Somebody in the news room had cut and pasted a couple of shots of Crispin together although – so far – there was little in the way of detail.

"Find out who he is." said Kranz. "And see what you can drum up in Europe. Start with our people in Austria."

Having worked with Kranz before, Al had already anticipated this suggestion and the news was far from good. Their usual collaborator in Vienna had recently become a long term resident of *Les Baumettes* and was unlikely to be free for the next 12 years.

"A pity," Kranz mumbled, remembering, perhaps, a friend as well as a colleague. "See if you can find some local people."

There was a small piece of paper in Al's hand, and it was here that he had scribbled down his orders when Kranz first called him in the small hours. Since then, he had been doing his homework and the news wasn't great. Clearing his throat to speak, Al raised an early concern.

"It's too fast!" he snapped, waving his notes. "The whole thing! You'll never make this schedule. Let 'em move on! Let 'em move down to London and we'll take 'em later on. Like we always do!"

But Kranz was in no mood to talk terms. He knew what was happening and he knew how to circumvent it. Releasing his finger from the mute button, he returned to the female voice in his ear.

"Which airport will you be flying to?"

"Just about any of them." He told her. "It's a small island."

Chapter 4

Alone on a small island, Crispin had finished his morning clinic and was looking forward to lunch. Strolling down a busy pavement, he glanced at an electrical store and noted a daytime chat show. There were three men in dickie bows and they were fighting it out on a pastel coloured sofa. In the absence of sound, Crispin didn't see much in it, but he should have done. All over the world, attention was shifting to the events of this morning and the possibility that one of the bed rocks of Western civilisation might turn out to be a completely different person from the one we always took him for.

But Crispin had other things on his mind. America is a big country and it was by no means certain what sort of American he was about to receive. Having said that, just about any sort of American would do, so long as they paid the rent. There were at least two spare bedrooms in his cottage, and if he managed to cope with his first lodger, he'd probably find a second one in the Spring.

Armed with a coffee and sandwich, Crispin decided to return to the clinic via the scenic route. In doing so, he passed the one single building that did more to drive down unemployment in Stratford than any other: *Shakespeare's Birthplace.* For some reason, the building was looking a bit darker than usual and Crispin felt an unexpected sense of schadenfreude. The roof on his own cottage was a lot sharper than Bill's.

Afternoon outpatients was pretty uneventful and by 6pm, Doctor Crispin Shakespeare was back in his hand-built speed machine and heading home. On the edge of the ring road, the traffic lights turned red and he took the opportunity to look to his right and check out the building site. Just short of the pavement, he spied a Defender style Land Rover with an iconic label,

BRITISH MUSEUM-ARCHAEOLOGY DEPARTMENT.

Crispin had no real need for a four-wheel drive, but he found himself drawn to the brutal, no nonsense face of the vehicle and wondered, absentmindedly, if he could bag one on e-bay and drive it up to Scotland. He adored his Morgan, but it was far too small for props and in a situation like this, he was more than willing to ignore his overdraft. In fact, had it not been for the Land Rover, Crispin might have given more attention to some of the other activities on the site. What he did notice, and what was obvious to his left, was a mass of smug media types, struggling to keep warm in the faint drizzle.

The lights turned green. The car roared forward and Crispin was soon surrounded by fields of golden hay. Tuning in to a commercial channel, he was surprised to hear his own name on the radio.

"There was excitement in Stratford today when a local doctor stumbled across a major archaeological find. Experts from the British Museum have been called and the site is surrounded by tight security. It seems that Doctor Crispin Shakespeare has uncovered what may turn out to be one of the most important discoveries of the century."

The news ended and the DJ returned with some nutty segue about his surname. Was Crispin related to the *real* Shakespeare? *No, dear listeners.* How could he be? *There was no male line.*

"Well, I'm glad we've got that straight," said Crispin, who had been coping with that one for most of the last twenty years. Turning left into a neat driveway, he pulled up to admire his truly sumptuous *thatched* cottage. Of all the homes in England, few would have fitted more comfortably on the lid of a chocolate box than this one. The building had caught his attention as a child and as an adult, he had been unable to resist the temptation to buy. But that was then. This was now. His mortgage lender was taking him to the cleaners and he was under considerable pressure to sell.

There was no aerial. Crispin hadn't watched television for quite some time and in any case, he much preferred the written word. More controversially, he had refused to install a burglar alarm. The insurance brokers were going crazy, but Crispin took a different view.

This building was not meant to be alarmed.

Collapsing into a fake leather armchair, he glanced up at a large monochrome photograph on the wall. In another man's home, it might have shown a scene from a wedding or a family gathering, but in Crispin's home, it portrayed a group of legless 19 year olds, livid besides a filthy paper towel machine in a Public Convenience.

Where were they now?

Actually, Crispin knew exactly where they were and it wasn't here, on the outskirts of a small market town in Warwickshire. Sometime soon, Jack would take leave of The Practice and it would be down to his nephew to seize the baton. Between now and that all-consuming day, what was there left for Crispin to do that he hadn't already done? Backpack around Asia? Get terribly good at Connect Four? Maybe, he could play on his membership of the TA and wrangle his way into a field hospital in Camp Bastion. He wasn't sure what Britain was doing in Afghanistan, or what good he could do when he got there, but at least he would be there. Where the action was.

It was time to get busy. Reaching for a pad of foolscap, Crispin scribbled a new title: 'Things to do'.

He wasn't the first man in history to write this list. There is a memorable sequence in *The Great Gatsby* that post dates Gatsby's life and introduces the reader to the previously unseen character of his father. The father has arrived in haste for Gatsby's funeral. Overcome by grief, he produces a crumpled 'jotter', where the eponymous nine-year-old had once penned his very own "to do list".

In this, the closing stages of a small masterpiece, the words of a child explain the nature of the man. There are people out there who despise Gatsby for the things he wrote on that book, but Crispin wasn't one of them. Maybe – just maybe – the world is divided into two camps. Those who see Gatsby as the hero of his own story and those who see him as the villain.

What then, might Crispin have put on that same page and how much of it might he put there now? Gaining a place in medical school was off. He'd already done that and the things we've already done never seem worth repeating.

Nothing came.

Why? Was he all out of ambitions? Whatever, Crispin was acutely aware of a pile of letters in his hallway and sorting them out seemed as good an excuse as any to avoid his list.

The first envelope contained a utility bill and Crispin decided to put it to one side. Next came a flyer for a course on *Expedition Medicine.* Somebody in Liverpool was trying to flog him a short course with a straight forward title. Crispin had never been to Liverpool and it wouldn't be as hard to access as Camp Bastion. Maybe he should give it a go.

But before he could get any further, a familiar name sprang up on his smartphone.

"*Tom!* I've been trying to ring you!"

Over in Cambridge University, a young and essentially unknown archaeologist was attempting to become known. His latest mad cap idea involved a dig on a Greek island and Tom began to explain his plan in detail.

Meanwhile, on Crispin's very own driveway, a single black taxi had just pulled up. Busy on the phone, Crispin totally missed the hand brake. Seconds later, the door opened and a shadowy figure from America egressed onto concrete.

"Where are we going?" asked Crispin.

"*Corfu*," Said Tom. "Wouldn't you just love to come along and dig something up?"

"Are you intending to pay me?"

"Not really," said Tom, who knew full well that he didn't need to.

"Will I get to snog the hot chick at the end? Like Harrison Ford?"

Tom moved towards the window of his historic office and reviewed the situation in the quad below. The ladies rowing team were marching for the Cam and Tom had managed to appoint himself as their official coach. They were, for the most part, the product of a privileged upbringing. How many of these idiots would be prepared to join him in Greece?

"You see, you've hit on a problem there." said Tom, his eyes fixed on his team. "There's never enough pretty girls to go around at these digs, and if anyone does get to snog them, I feel very strongly it should be me."

Crimping the phone beneath his chin, Crispin tore open the next envelope. At the very top of the page, somebody had written the words, 'BANK STATEMENT'. After that it got worse.

"Actually, I don't need money anymore. I've got this American bloke…" Interrupted by the bell, Crispin was forced to say sorry, adding, "Hang on a minute, this could really save my neck."

He turned the handle and a charming young lady from America appeared on the doorstop, fully equipped with designer luggage.

"I'll call you back." Said Crispin, taping the red button. "You're not the American are you?"

She was. Lucy was blonde, smiling and optimistic.

"Yes," said Crispin, becoming hesitant. "Are you familiar with the word, *actress*?"

Whilst she was, Lucy suffered from the very firm conviction that, "Actress is so passé."

"I'm terribly sorry, but I was led to believe that you were…"

"A man?"

Yes, that was what he had been led to believe, but the ac*tor* in question had already reached the staircase and showed little in the way of hesitation. "This is great!" He heard her shout from the landing, "Can you see that Shakespeare theatre from here?"

"No," said Crispin, with real conviction.

"Which one of these rooms is mine?"

Abandoned in the hallway, Crispin scrambled after her.

"You see, this mattress just isn't strong enough to take a woman with your habitus."

Too late! Lucy had checked her room and was charging back down.

"Are you suggesting I'm fat?"

"No." said Crispin. "I'm just confessing to the true state of my furniture." Then he added, "In fact, that's my second best bed."

But there was worse to come. His bank statement was waiting on the sofa and Lucy snatched the thing up on sight.

"Hey!" shouted Crispin.

"Wait a minute! Wait a minute! One of these pound things is worth more than a dollar? Right?"

This was a challenge to his patriotic spirit and Crispin responded in kind. "*Of course!*"

"How much more?"

"These days?" The doctor shrugged, slightly less sure of himself. "About thirty pence."

"Great!" said Lucy, fanning her face with his overdraft. "Because that means you're even more desperate than I thought you were!"

"Well, I wouldn't say *desperate*."

"Well, how would you describe it, Doctor Crispin Shakespeare, account number 98076–"

"I'd say, I have a lot of earnings potential."

"When you say *po-ten-ti-al*, are you talking about the stuff you haven't got yet?"

This was true.

"Look, I am Lucy Bernstein. I am 26 years old and I'm not spending another day in that shitty little bed and breakfast they left me in since March. Do you want to make me one of those cups of tea that are supposed to be so English? God knows why! They probably grow the stuff in Kenya!

Most of her luggage was still in the hallway and Crispin decided to help her take it up. As luggage goes, it was better than some and Crispin couldn't help but marvel at some of the labels. Your average actor - he knew - just doesn't have a lot of readies.

"You bought this stuff off the stage?"

The actress smiled a wholesome smile, noting,

"I have friends in high places."

Lucy began to unpack and tea in itself has never taken that long to prepare. Alone on the ground floor, Crispin had been anything but idle and a bona-fide log fire was soon blazing in the front room. It might have been easier to turn on the gas, but Crispin loved the feel of a real fire, and in Lucy's mind, this was a fairy tale vision of the place she had come to find.

That been said, the bookcase seemed more exciting to her than the fire.

"What's this?" Lucy had spotted Crispin's latest work for the stage and read the title out loud: "*Learning by Humiliation?*"

"It's mine. Incredibly, I am a writer. I write for an amateur troupe."

"What? Like the real guy?"

"Yes," said Crispin. "Exactly like him."

"Like, if he was really real. You're known, they're not even sure who William Shakespeare was. How can you be sure of anything? He might have been *gay*."

Whilst Crispin Shakespeare was antagonised, he was able to retain his composure. "Unlikely."

"He might have been a woman."

"Impossible," he told her, much more loudly.

"He might have been American."

"Oh, for God's sake!" shouted Crispin. "That's down right offensive!"

But his lodger was only laughing and they would both be at work in the morning.

Chapter 5

In the course of rehearsal, a play becomes much more than a wad of pages. It is a living thing. It is a fresh and original exercise in English Comprehension and on the production front, the modern day director will always face the same challenge: *how can I make my version of Julius Caesar any different from all the others?*

This year at the RSC, the man with the big challenge was supported by his long suffering assistant, Gordon, who had attended an earlier rehearsal in a cravat but who arrived today wearing something much more conventional. At the far end of the stage, Caesar himself was barefoot in jeans, T-shirt and the kind of broad white bed sheet that can easily double as a toga.

Right on cue, Caesar chanted from a well-known text:
*"Cowards die many times before their deaths;
The valiant never taste of death but once."*

This was good, solid stuff, but it wasn't the only show in town. A short walk across the Avon, Crispin's ragtag collection of wannabes had assembled in the Village Hall, and were about to rehearse from their very own text. As usual, the players here would be performing under the same name they had adopted as Medical Students: *The Cunning Linguists*.

Ten feet short of the stage, their self appointed leader was relaxed in a simple wooden chair. A little to his left, his friend Duncan, was ready to run forward.

Duncan had the unmistakable airs and graces of an off duty medic, and in his day job, he had developed a passion for upper GI endoscopy that sometimes left Crispin confused. Having wrapped himself in a vast white coat, Duncan was sported the kind of eyebrows that would have been better suited to the young Dennis Healy. But Dennis Healey had been dead and buried for some years now and Duncan really ought to have had them cut back.

Approaching stage right, the far more placid figure of Sarah was co-starring as his faithful nurse.

Sarah pointed to a doctor's bag and Harry, a 28-year-old psychiatrist, listened with fake interest. Fully equipped in a beige jacket, Harry was a model of middle-class restraint.

"If you're a psychiatrist," demanded Sarah, "why are you carrying those gynaecological instruments?"

"What gynaecological instruments?" demanded Harry, his voice shrill with the excitement of it all.

A dull canvas bag fell open on stage and a bundle of steel tongues clanged against the floor. Crispin turned on the music and Harry flipped into his song and dance routine.

Meanwhile, over at the RSC, things were a bit more mainstream. Crispin's lodger was addressing Caesar in the guise of his wife, *Calpurnia.*

"Alas my Lord, your wisdom is consumed…"

It was good line, well delivered, but strangely tainted by a foreign accent. Jumping to his feet, the RSC director was the first to pass judgement. "Can I just make one thing clear," he swiped. "The wife of Julius Caesar's is not and never will be a resident of the California. *This* is the Royal Shakespeare Company!"

"Well, why is she speaking English at all?" asked Calpurnia. "Isn't it supposed to be Ancient Greece!"

"Rome!" called Gordon, stating the obvious.

Centre stage, the RSC director had progressed to a new base line emotion: *rage*. Still on the level, his camp assistant showed a surprising aptitude for *collusion*, asking, "Do you really think she's ready for a Stratford production?"

Boldly and as if Lucy wasn't there, the director agreed. "My thoughts exactly," he said. "What about that thatched thing they've built by the Thames?"

"*The Globe?*"

"Yes," said the director, in frank agreement. "*The Globe*. I hear it's full of splendid foreign tourists."

Six feet ahead of him, his leading lady was unimpressed, shrieking, "What is wrong with this place? Do you think there aren't any tourists in Stratford?"

"It's all a matter of style," said Caesar, refusing to raise his voice. "There's simply no excuse for pretending to be American."

"Well, what if you really *are* American!"

"Even then," said Caesar, heading towards a minefield. "I mean, just look at Gwyneth Paltrow."

"Gwyneth Paltrow!" wailed Lucy. "Gwyneth Paltrow! All I ever hear is Gwy-neth-blood-y-Palt-trow."

"Well, I found her completely convincing in Shakespeare in Love," said the director, sneering very loudly whilst he stormed towards the edge of the stage, lost his footing and crashed three feet to the ground.

But this kind of spontaneity was petty compared to the scene in the Village Hall. Less than two hundred yards from The Swan, Harry's barmy dance routine was gathering speed. The music was modern and unlicensed but with the kind of venue The Linguists were planning to hire, copyright wouldn't be an issue. Moments later, Harry's performance came to a sudden halt when he tripped on his own stethoscope and made his way to the floor.

"Good fall!" said Crispin, a tad short on empathy. "Good fall! You looked like you were in real pain there."

Harry made a peculiar burping noise whilst nobody tried to help. In any case, Crispin's mobile was going loud and a foul mood descended upon the Hall.

"Are you *on call*?" asked Sarah.

"It's alright," said Crispin, which was his own way of saying *yes*. "This is Shakespeare's birthplace. Nothing ever happens on a Saturday."

They were all medics and they all understood, but that didn't make it any easier. Crispin collected his own, prestigious looking doctor's bag and ambled, casually to the back door and so on to an ancient bridge that led out across the Avon. A few minutes later, he was standing in the strange and other world of the RSC rehearsal rooms, where a bunch of proper actors had gathered around his patient.

Akinetic on the floor, the RSC director was showing his troupe how to do it.

"Doctor! I could see a light! I saw a light in the darkness!"

Crispin turned to his lodger and asked for more detail.

"Did he lose consciousness?"

"No," said Lucy, with the kind of bluntness that can cost a girl dearly. "He just fell off the edge and started sobbing."

Crispin produced his pen torch and spun the thing from one orbit to the next.

"I can see a light," said the RSC director, who really could.

Three feet to the left, Gordon the assistant director had gotten as far as *soothing*. "It's alright, Peter," he said, soothingly. "Doctor Shakespeare is an excellent doctor."

A cold silence engulfed the theatre and the man on the floor showed unexpected signs of vigour.

"*Shakespeare?*" he exclaimed. "Aren't you the same idiot who dug up those books?"

"Yes," said Crispin, in a smug, self congratulatory sort of way. "That's me."

"Well, I'd just like to say, I find your activities completely disgusting."

Crispin said something upbeat about the search for truth and the dispersal of human knowledge, but the director had other ideas.

"I've already published *the* definitive biography of the Bard! If you are suggesting that that man could have known anything about his own life that I haven't already inferred, you're completely deluded!"

Crispin presented a single digit to the director's face and invited him to count.

"Two," said the director, deliberately lying.

Two was as good an answer as any and Crispin returned his pen torch to his bag and pretended to be deaf, whilst Gordon started hissing in his boss's ear.

"I think you dealt with him very well. He won't be making any more great discoveries in a hurry!"

Lucy asked Crispin about the need for stitches and Crispin reassured her that the director hadn't actually cut himself, so no, there wasn't any. But Lucy's problems ran much deeper than mild concussion. They extended to the ruler of the known world.

"Oh, I wouldn't worry about him," said Crispin. "He can't even beat Cassius at the breast stroke. Look, I've got to get back to my rehearsal, but later this evening, my cast and I will be sharing a drink in one of the few taverns still accessible to the public."

"Is it The Dog and Duck?"

It *was* The Dog and Duck, and he didn't need to linger and draw a map. Instead, Crispin left the theatre, a little more slowly than he had arrived. Plodding to the Village Hall, he walked past one of the many designer clothing stores that gave depth to the High Street. Ordinarily, a town of this size could never have attracted a brand of this quality but, as Crispin well knew, this was no ordinary town. This was Stratford Upon Avon.

And it was at that very second that Tom decided to buzz him by text. Tom had spent the day on the River Cam, doing his best to coach a bunch of female rowers.

"I'm getting increasingly turned on by all the Hephzibahs, Charlottes and Anastasias, the sweat glistened victorious rowing team, hugging each other. Bankside. In their Navy Blue shorts. And their powerful thighs. And plaited long hair. I wish they'd stop."

Tom's team had just defeated a major rival and he was about to take them to the local watering hole for a post-match de-brief. Knowing Tom, this was unlikely to be anything more than a massive piss up and Crispin took time to type his condolences onto cold glass, "*I feel for you mate, I really do,*" and then press *send.*

In the circumstances, this was about as much sympathy as he could offer and Crispin took care to pocket his smartphone before it could distract him anymore. As he did so, he felt something else. It was the sheet of paper he had salvaged from the cellar. Doing his best to look innocent, Crispin unfolded the paper in the street and checked its fading scrawl.

Maybe he should have salvaged two sheets rather than one? No, it was an important document and it wasn't his place to interpret the find. On the other hand, keeping this one single page wouldn't change the course of history, so he wasn't exactly wracked by guilt. At least, not yet.

Returning the paper to his pocket, he decided to look through the shop window. Like most of the big names on the High Street, this one hired a fresh batch of models every season, but as far as Crispin could make out, they were always the same. 'Slim but never bony. Fair but never really blonde. For a brand where fashion is based on self-restraint, these people startled mostly for being conventional.

And what about Lucy? Was his lodger likely to spend her hard earned money in this store? No. The only woman he expected to see in here was Sarah, and Sarah was just one of his troupe.

Chapter 6

But the floral patterned dress shop was just the tip of the iceberg. From an economic perspective, Stratford is a one trick pony. The legacy of a single dead son has kept the populace in house and home for most of the last two hundred years and without him, the entire economy would, presumably, implode. It's debatable whether the Bard's men ever performed here, but the feel and the verve of the place is enough to convince your average punter that they might have done and Stratford remains the most visited literary shrine in England.

Central to the whole set up are the theatres, the largest of these being The Swan. Resplendent in the wake of its modern refurbishment, the theatre we see today dates back to the 1930s and was supported by a vigorous fund raising campaign in the United States. A row of xenon lights help to boost the ambience and make it a grand day out for everyone involved, even the kind of person who knows nothing at all about the Bard. Bill can pack 'em in morning, noon and night, and right up until the day when Crispin tried his hand at abseiling, it had never occurred to anyone that it might end.

And yet it had. A previously nondescript construction site had been transformed. Grass and builder's rubble had given way to military style tents, and when night came, free standing floodlights blazed down from the heavens.

Heroic, at the bottom of the sink hole, men in blue cagoules were ferreting through the mud, hell bent on some second – even more astonishing – discovery. Meanwhile, up on the surface, all the world's journalists had assembled on a nearby pavement, where the British climate came close to trouncing them every half hour. The north side of the site backed out onto a dry stonewall and on the east side, there was the main warehouse of the RSC. It was true that security had been upgraded, but it was true also that the show simply must go on and the RSC stage hands had retained access to their props.

All this excitement had not gone unnoticed in the rest of the town. Less than a hundred yards away, The Dog and Duck was brimming over with the usual crowd and at this very moment, each and every one of them was staring at a 50 inch plasma screen on the wall.

"It's been three days since the unexpected find in Stratford. Earlier today, our reporter spoke to the man responsible for this fortuitous discovery, Doctor Crispin Shakespeare."

The fortuitous figure in question flashed up on the screen and the entire room burst into song.

"The man was in the hole," said Crispin. "I looked to one side and I saw some boxes." Somebody pressed him to comment on the significance of the find, but the doctor had other ideas. "Not so great as the very latest Shakespearean play to grace the Edinburgh Festival, *Learning by Humiliation*. An entirely new production by our greatest living playwright!"

It was a plug that went down better in The Dog and Duck than it did with the press. Crispin's lead actor, Duncan, for example, found it positively hilarious and few of the revellers in this place would have bothered to argue with him. At six foot three, Duncan was about as wide as some of these people were tall. In medical school, he had rowed - very successfully - in the first eight and if you waited by the Avon at the break of the day, you could still spot him on the water, speeding along in the cox-less fours. Even now, hauling three pints around the bar, he seemed to be presenting a sporting trophy.

What did he think of that?

"Very fortuitous!"

But there was more going on in Stratford than drinking. Unbeknown to the regulars in the Dog and Duck, a brown Hertz car was fast approaching the ring road. Having arrived just after lunch, Kranz had spent the afternoon checking into his pre-booked bed and breakfast. There, some grovelling, small time hotelier had helped him find a towel and an ironing board and directed him to the village shop where he could buy a comb and the sort of tiny tube of toothpaste that can still make it through airport security. Such was the urgency of his flight from the States that his hand held and battered leather suitcase had been packed in real haste and lacked these basic pleasures. All in all, it had been a hearty welcome from an old country and by the time Arthur Kranz returned to his vehicle, the hotel manager felt certain that he was as good an egg as any.

Shortly after dark, the Hertz car arrived at the building site. There, a solitary police officer bent double to check his documents. Arthur Kranz was an expected international dignitary and the officer on the gate was in no mood to slow his progress. Driving a little further, Arthur saw a tiny blue and white ribbon that straddled both alleyways. British security, he noted, wasn't all it was cracked up to be.

He played with the Sat Nav and blew up the image. Using technology that the first Elizabethans could never have dreamt of, Kranz was able to determine not just his own location, but that of every exit in the area, as well as the nearby canal. The all important RSC warehouse, with its wide unloading bay, was a short distance to his right.

In addition, and although it didn't appear on the screen, Arthur had already noticed Crispin's absurd wooden plaything, prominent besides a dry stonewall. The factory in Malvern knocked out less than a dozen machines a week and it seemed unlikely that there were two British Racing Green Morgans in Stratford.

Then, right on cue, there was movement. To Arthur's total delight, a long, white lorry pulled up beside the barrier and a dumpy little policewoman stepped out of her box and asked to see ID. The driver shrugged and said that he didn't have any and the policewoman giggled, idiotically and waved him through.

Exiting the car with the air of an innocent, Arthur advanced towards the tents. In front of him, a bright, red notice had been pinned to a tree: NO UNAUTHORISED VEHICLES BEYOND THIS POINT.

Arthur Kranz had driven here complete with his own costume: a checkered Popeye hat, mirrored spectacles and a mauve trench coat. In the cloistered world of academic archaeology, his was a known name and Kranz was quickly lauded on sight by his British counterpart. A short while later, a second Brit appeared out of nowhere, fully equipped with a moustache and a strange stoop. Shaking Kranz by the hand, he waxed lyrical about the joy of this moment.

Was Kranz comfortable? Had he found a reasonable place to stay? Arthur Kranz had, and then the man with the moustache smiled and asked what part of the excavation he would like to see first.

"I'd like to see the books."

Whilst all this was happening, The Cunning Linguists had taken over an entire table in The Dog and Duck. Crispin's stint on the television was fading rapidly and in its place came a cruel and ugly mood.

"What's the matter?" he asked, trying to sound reasonable.

The man with the Denis Healy eyebrows was deadly serious. Grabbing a pad of printed foolscap, he pressed one finger against the title,

LEARNING BY HUMILIATION

"It's just not good enough," he said, jeering very slightly.

On a better day, Crispin might have looked to Sarah for support but tonight, she was siding with his opponents. Pointing at Crispin's script, she moved in for the kill. "It's *not* funny."

"The problem," said Harry, "is that it's too much of a take on your own life."

"Well, that's what writers do," Crispin retorted. "They look for source material in their own experience base."

"Not necessarily," said Sarah, doing her best to sound difficult. "You can make stuff up."

"Chekov did," perked Duncan.

Crispin had never really seen himself as a Chekov connoisseur, but if Duncan was digressing, then there was hope.

"Chekov *what*?" he asked, trying to drag it out.

"Chekov said that the lines he gave to his characters had nothing to do with his own beliefs," said Duncan. "He said that writers invent their own storylines."

"And Chekov was friends with Stanislavski,"

"And Stanislavski was a real big shot."

"Do any of you people even know how to pronounce *Stanislavski*?" moaned Crispin, who didn't know either.

But Duncan refused to give up.

"What this script needs, is carefully crafted spontaneity!"

"Less of this bored family doctor stuff," jibed Harry, "and more of the rip-roaring ward based dialogue. Comedy wet with the morning dew."

"*Wet with the morning dew?*" griped Crispin. "What the hell is comedy wet with the morning dew? Look! I have been taking you to Scotland for what? Five, maybe six years?"

"Seven years."

"Seven years!" said Crispin, as if he'd just remembered, "To *great* acclaim."

"But we've never won anything!" moaned the girl. "When we were kids, you told us we were going to bag a prize."

When they were kids. 'Good line. A mere seven years ago, they were describing themselves as kids. Now, they were adult doctors facing untold responsibilities on a daily basis. The central thrust of Sarah's accusation was, however, beginning to make its mark. As a medical student, Crispin had promised them that they would go to Edinburgh and win a prize. They never had. And it was at this point, that the God of small time comedy took pity on

Crispin and decreed that his lodger, Lucy should enter the room.

"Harry," grunted Crispin, nodding in the right direction. "It's *Lucy*. This is Lucy."

The psychiatrist looked up and stood, very promptly to shake her hand. "Delighted a lot," said Harry, who really was.

Secure in her seat, Sarah spoke as if the lodger was still outside.

"Is she like a creative muse? Crispin! Only you could have found a muse to fix your overdraft."

But Sarah was a lone voice of dissent. The RSC actress was a sure fire hit and was drawing attention from all directions. Having escaped the threat of a full-scale mutiny, Crispin wondered what else she would be good for. Quite possibly, he should try and market a major cosmetic product using her brand. Maybe a fragrance? Image wise, he could see it now. A grainy shot of Lucy in the RSC dressing room, flirting with some unseen Ralph Fiennes type by the mirrors.

Spirit of Lucy Bernstein. New York blonde in the West Midlands.

She'd be the hottest thing this side of Smethwick. If he could pick up five per cent as her agent, he'd make more on their first photo shoot than he'd ever squeeze out of Jack.

"To Doctor Crispin Shakespeare," said Harry, proposing a toast. "Soon to give us the most dazzling show ever to hit the Edinburgh stage."

They rang for last orders and when the ringing was over, the actress raised another issue.

"Are you related to Bill?"

"No," said Crispin, with deep patience. "The Shakespeare family died out years ago. Or at least *his* did."

Lucy showed interest in the Bard and Crispin provided more depth.

"There are only eleven written documents that make direct reference to Shakespeare's life. Apart from the plays, obviously. And the poems. There's plenty of hard evidence that he existed, but very little detail as to who he was. At some stage, there was this visiting Swiss tourist, who broke off to watch a few of his plays. Then the Swiss guy wrote a letter home, saying what a great time he was having in London, going to the theatre. Also, there's an inscription in the Church where they buried him, written by his cast. And that's about it."

She asked how he knew so much about the Bard and Crispin did his best to hide his surprise. He was an educated thinking person, he could read and he had done.

"There are people out there who don't even think he wrote them," said Lucy, reminding him of a well known theory. "Every kid who wants to be smart gets pushed to read some Shakespeare and Shakespeare might not even be the guy who wrote them. Imagine that!" Crispin, could imagine that and he found the whole thing pretty alarming. "Some people," she persisted, "think it might have been Elizabeth the First."

The Virgin Queen, said Crispin, was an unlikely candidate. "It takes time to write," he explained, with real confidence. "So, he got through thirty-six plays and some sonnets? The Head of State just didn't have that kind of time on her hands. Even if she had the brain – and she probably did have the brain – she would have been too busy running the country. It was Bill, alright. Believe me!"

But Lucy had stopped listening. Over on the television, the previously unknown figure of *Larry O'Neil*, was about to do a piece to camera and the words, 'IRISH LITERARY EXPERT', were there beneath his face.

"We can be certain of this," said O'Neil. "Shakespeare wasn't from Stratford Upon Avon at all. As is discussed in my book..."

Seizing his chance, O'Neil held up a copy of his very own pamphlet: *WAS SHAKESPEARE IRISH?*

"The greatest writer in the English language was in fact, a God faring Catholic from County Cork. And as soon as the new documents are made public, I feel strongly that my thesis will be vindicated. In the meantime, and for one week only, your viewers are invited to buy my book at a 'specially discounted rate."

In an unusual sop to commerciality, the subtitles faded and the link to the relevant web page leapt up on the screen.

Ten feet from the bar, Crispin had a go at *flippant*.

"Shakespeare is alive and well!" he shouted. "And working as a deck chair attendant in Margate. He's with Elvis. They're both claiming disability payments for back pain, even though there's nothing wrong with them."

But Crispin had badly misjudged the public mood. The regulars in The Dog and Duck were more than despondent and the man behind the bar was completely incensed.

"You're not gonna be very welcome round here!" he barked. "Not if that one turns out right! What have we got in Stratford 'cept them tourists?"

Out of view, some other nameless half-wit tried to second the motion. "The tourists will be off to Cork!"

The tourists will be off to Cork!

A dull echo swept around the bar and in that same instant, Crispin's one time colleague, Duncan, stepped forward with his smart phone and a finger on mute. "It's for *you*," he mumbled. "Some media types want to hear your views on the Irish Question. Where will you be in the morning? Isn't it 1, the Thatched something?"

"No," said Crispin, after the briefest of delays. "Just tell them 23, The Stables."

Five years in the first eight hadn't damaged Duncan's connection with his roots. Switching to the kind of working-class candour he did so well, he relayed Crispin's message to the unsuspecting hack on the phone. "That's 23 the Stables mate," he cried. "Yes, first thing tomorrow morning! And don't be late."

Chapter 7

But tomorrow was some distance away and Arthur Kranz had just set eyes on the most seductive object on this planet. Having been transferred to the central marquee, the contents of the boxes had been left on an improvised bench and spread out across a dull grey tablecloth.

Two feet above their heads, a single 60 watt light bulb swung slowly from an electrical cable. Frustrated by his own shadow, Arthur grabbed the bulb in one hand and refused to let go.

A few of the better preserved volumes had been wrapped in black plastic and were awaiting transfer to London. Another volume looked to be in an advanced state of decay and it seemed unlikely that its contents would be viable.

Over to Arthur's right, a British academic had raised his magnifying glass and was about to start reading. Completing an entire sentence, Peter Bainbridge PhD spoke very softly to himself.

"*My goodness!*"

Cold and entirely serious, Arthur checked the guy's ID badge and asked for first impressions.

"Most of them seem to be ledgers," said Bainbridge. "Financial records."

"Records of what?" demanded Kranz, just that little bit too quickly.

"Of the theatre."

There were, Kranz reminded them, a great many theatres in England. How could he be sure?

"Oh, it's the Globe," laughed Bainbridge. "And it doesn't last any longer than his career. So, the timing's bang on."

For Arthur Kranz, this was a pivotal moment. Should he stay here as a visiting Professor from the States or should he leave as a recognised art thief? It was a difficult and life changing decision, and in thick of it, Bainbridge did everything he could to help.

"The volumes over here haven't been opened." he explained. "One of them looks beyond salvage. But *this* material is getting us *very* excited..."

Even as Bainbridge spoke, Kranz's mind was heading elsewhere. Specifically: *the guards.* On his left, he saw an older man in a dark blue uniform and Kranz could sense the boredom on his face. If Arthur Kranz waited a little longer, then the vulnerability of this site might yet increase, but if he waited too long, the Museum might transfer this entire find to London.

A heist at the British Museum was an altogether greater challenge and there was unlikely to be a second opportunity to match the one he faced today. Arthur placed a hand in his pocket, and began to touch his smartphone, tapping as he did, a virtual tab. The phone quivered and the game was on.

Back in the real world, Bainbridge had gotten as far as imaging. Staff from the Museum had assembled an elaborate photographic rig and positioned an open book beneath its lens.

"Well, I must say, Doctor Kranz, this really is a thrill. Domestic archaeology isn't like Greece. 'Not for us anyway. Whenever we find anything, we usually end up in the same peat bog on Dartmoor. You see," he continued, "if you look over here, you'll notice that we've been photographing the manuscript, page by page. The big boys in London wanted us to wait until we'd reached the Museum, but I couldn't resist the temptation."

As an archaeologist, Bainbridge was not a criminal investigator. If he had been, he might have read more into the next question.

"What are you up to?"

"What page?" asked Bainbridge. Kranz nodded. "28. I know that doesn't sound very much, but it's a very meticulous process. We're worried about fragility."

"And are they? Fragile?"

"Actually, no. Some of these pages here are remarkably well preserved. You could carry them off in your knapsack if you wanted to! Do you remember that time when they found the Mary Rose?"

By coincidence, Kranz was a recognised expert on that matter.

"Well, in the Solent, they tried to blame the mud. The mud preserved the timber. But for this find, I'd put my money on the air. They were totally sealed in, you see. Dry air turns out to be better than wet mud! Especially for paper."

Kranz moved closer to an open manuscript and Bainbridge continued.

"We've got people prizing the thing apart, page by page. Or at least we did have until they all went back to their hotels." The archaeologist laughed, manically. "I think the TV people are packing up too! Come back tomorrow," he said, doing his best to sound sober. "and I'll give you the full tour."

But as far as Arthur was concerned, there wasn't going to be any tomorrow. His orders were already out there and it was impossible to bring them back. A mile or so down the river, an inflatable black dinghy had slipped its moorings and begun its approach to the town. Both outboards had been carefully muffled with polystyrene hoods and a couple of men in black balaclava helmets were steady besides the wheel. It was a journey that took them past a hundred waterfront properties and in the days that followed, many of the owners would claim to have heard their tune. Few, if any of them, reacted at the time.

Over in the Marquee, Bainbridge had gotten as far as the Renaissance. "We have a very similar situation with Leonardo de Vinci," he continued. "The body of work bequeathed by that guy was amazing, but we don't really know who he was. Did he go to Art School? Was he self-taught? We haven't a clue. You know, De Vinci did some anatomical sketches and planned to publish them while he was still alive. In the end, he died very suddenly and they ended up stuck on a shelf for about two hundred years. If he'd been quicker off the mark, medicine might have been two centuries ahead of itself."

Bainbridge laughed again, an excited, eager man who had just discovered the find of a life time. Turning his back to Kranz, he was all but defenceless and a second or two later, a clenched fist collided with his skull. Bainbridge hit the ground with one almighty thud and Kranz spun around, looking for the security guard and seeing nothing. Disposing of Bainbridge first, the American slid his body across the floor, eventually dumping it on the edge of the tent.

There was no time to lose. Dashing to the wall of the Marquee, Kranz flung back a white tarpaulin and saw – to his undisguised joy – a brick wall with a large gap in the middle. Stepping through the gap, he looked out across the canal. The anatomy of the dig, the Marquee and the canal had been set up with this operation in mind and if everything went to plan, the dinghy would be here in a matter of minutes.

Arthur Kranz returned to the table and encountered the same bloated security guard who had been here before. Although conscious that Bainbridge had vanished, this man was not yet alerted and Kranz brought him down with a single blow to his jaw. It was – perhaps - a harder landing than Kranz had planned for and for the security guard, it would prove his last. Blood oozed out onto the flattened grass and Kranz was quick to wipe the spray from his coat. Unfolding his handkerchief quite slowly, he checked, very carefully for stains. Finding none, he stuffed it into a trouser pocket and set off in search of his books.

Chapter 8

Oblivious to the drama down the road, The Cunning Linguists were living it up in the pub and doing their best to annoy Lucy.

"Tell us, Lucy baby," smirked Harry, "tell, us, what brings you to this far flung corner of the world."

"I'm here for the work," she explained, without any real enthusiasm. "How about you?"

"I'm here for the psychopaths."

"Harry does psych," said Crispin, in brisk translation. "He's a psychiatrist."

"Do you get a lot of psychopaths in these parts?" asked Lucy.

"You'd be surprised," said Harry, doing ominous. "And what else brings you here?"

"I guess I was running away." For the first time since Crispin had met her, she actually sound vulnerable. "I was running away, too."

"Man trouble," said Sarah, not as a question.

"Man trouble," came the dull repetition from a jobbing actress.

In the lexicon of female love, Sarah told them, *Man* is a recognised synonym for *trouble.*

"Wait a minute, wait a minute," blurted Crispin, "I don't accept that!"

"Arthur!" moaned Lucy. "Arthur Kranz! Part-time art dealer, part-time college professor, full-time bastard!"

Crispin felt the need to hear more but his cast were running away with themselves, discarding the script and inventing their own lines. Ten minutes ago, he was getting hammered for bad writing. Now he was a celebrated literary genius. The only difference between then and now was the presence of a pretty girl in a pub and he decided to bring her more often.

Later, Lucy and Sarah disappeared to the ladies' room and Harry became difficult.

"So, how are you doing?" asked Harry, annotating the question with a dirty wink.

"In what sense?" said Crispin.

"Have you given any thought to what sort of girl she is?"

"What sort is she?"

"Well, I doubt if she takes any prisoners in bed. I'd make a move myself, but I'm still holding myself in reserve for Kristen Scott Thomas!"

Crispin's facial expression changed abruptly and Harry much preferred the new one.

The two of them turned to their left and saw Lucy and Sarah, emergent but still out of range.

"You're sure she's really called Lucy?"

"Yes!" snapped Crispin. "Why the heck would she not be?"

"Well she's an actress. They're always changing their names. Have you gone on google yet? Maybe she isn't a real person!"

Crispin hadn't, nor for that matter did he take kindly to this latest suggestion.

"Harry," said Crispin, very sternly. "I'm a highly trained man. I am a member of an elite military unit."

"*Part time*, elite military unit," said Harry, who was like that.

"I am a playwright and a fully qualified physician."

"The playwright thing is the bit that would get me worried."

"Nothing fazes me."

The women returned in tandem, conscious that other people had been waiting. Harry had been raised in a privileged environment and queues had never really featured in his life. "How very working class," he muttered, leading the way to the door and the world outside.

The troupe broke up, with Harry, Sarah and Duncan drifting South across the river and Crispin and the lodger heading North. Parking isn't easy in a tourist trap and Crispin had been forced to leave the Morgan some distance from the pub. On the way, he started to ramble about his uncle, their shared practice and the widely accepted prophesy that the nephew should inherit the Earth. Or at least, the family business. A few days ago, this kind of frankness would have been hard to imagine, and it wasn't just the lager. In Crispin's experience, the night itself can ease the tongue. But Lucy wasn't interested. Lucy had picked up on a wise crack from the boys in the bar and mulled it over in her head.

"How very working class?" He heard her quirk. "So, what class are you?"

"Ascending," said Crispin, without any sense of irony, "You see, my father was a writer."

"And what class is that?"

"It's about as low as you can get without actually being dead. In fact, as far as I can make out, he died a borderline pauper. 'Had to leave it to his only son to rise to the noble status of Family Doctor. Eventually," he continued, "I hope to become an aristocrat."

Crispin's speed machine was exactly where he had left it, British Racing Green and just short of the fluttering police banner. What he barely noticed, but what would later become so completely clear, was the position of the RSC lorry. Ten yards away and on the other side of the blue and white ribbon, the doors to a long white container were wide open.

And it was at this same instant that Arthur emerged from the Marquee. Straining with the physical burden of his haul, he leaned against the lorry and tried to catch his breath. As he had expected, several packing cases were there on the floor, all of them ready for loading. Arthur picked one up and raised it to the level of the container. Pushing his booty further in, he looked to his right and saw a young couple beneath an orange street light, neatly framed by the blackened walls of the alley. It was a vision that delayed him for the best part of three seconds. Then he returned to the box, using his feet to slide it in some more. A reference number had been stencilled onto unpainted plywood and Kranz mouthed this sequence to himself in the darkness: "*RSC119.*"

Moments later, he was back on the cobbles and back on his feet with little more than a damp patch on one knee to show for his troubles. Hearing a familiar laugh, Arthur froze all over again, hiding behind the lorry and willing her to stop.

If Crispin and Lucy dragged this exchange out any longer, Arthur's entire strategy might have broken down, but as fate might have it, their time by the Morgan would be brief.

Lucy grabbed Crispin's smart phone and prepared to take a shot.

"Lemme take a picture of you by the car," she cried.

But Crispin already knew just how ugly he really was and asked instead that he might steal a shot of her. Retrieving his phone in haste, he played with a touch sensitive screen and watched, entranced, as the actress reacted to the lens.

"Hi Mum," He heard her call.

She was in England. She was living in sin with an aspiring aristocrat. She was blonde, she was above average height, and she was invincible as Crispin had been, just a few short years ago.

Holed up behind the lorry, Arthur waited for them to drive away and then escaped the scene himself, upright, very slowly and on foot. Standing at the checkpoint, he made a point of speaking to the dumpy woman police officer where they moaned about the weather together and discussed the contents of his briefcase. Hiding his disappointment when she refused to look inside, Arthur chatted at length with the last dregs of a CNN crew. It was cold and their rivals had already run to the bar, but these guys were still out here and eager to grab some footage whenever they got the chance. Kranz was, after all, a recognised expert in this field.

What was he doing here? What had they found? Could he come back in the morning and do it all again? Sure. He would be better dressed in the morning and better rested from his traipse across the pond. Smiling for the only camera in sight, Arthur heard the drone of a distant outboard and consciously failed to react.

The interview ended and Arthur went back to his Hertz car and started driving north. Turning right at a prominent road sign, he pulled up beside a wall of dense foliage and remembered to kill the lights. The canal was only a few feet away and he moved towards the towpath where he stripped to his underwear and burnt everything else he had on. There was a complete change of clothing in the boot and a forecast of rain in the night. When the Sun rose in the morning, there would be nothing to say he had even been here.

A few miles away, Winston and Al had cleared the town and were dousing down the dinghy with petrol. Fire will always confound the forensics and the entire towpath was soon alight. Arthur's men escaped to a waiting transit van and, in less than an hour, they were offloading in Redditch whilst their driver, Gary, pushed on for the M6. If his luck didn't hold, then the police might link him to the crime, but even if they did, then there would be nothing in the vehicle that could ever be seen as evidence.

Gary liked that. As a third generation criminal, he had learnt his trade from his father and his grandfather and none of them had spent a lot of time inside. Thieves don't advertise in The Yellow Pages and Al had gained his contact details from a previous associate in Brixton.

Ginger to the last hair on his head, Gary had long understood that Shakespeare was waste of time. In Gary's mind, Shakespeare was about as much use as algebra and like everything else he had learnt in school, algebra had been of no use to him at all in this life. When it came to his contract, Gary only had one rule: whatever he stole, it had to be worthless. Portraiture, the occasional sculpture, maybe even a few precious stones. But never food, or cash, or household goods. Nothing that might have value to the common man. Like his grandparents, Gary had long believed that your average household burglar should be shot. Gary's clan were like that. They would never have stolen from their own brethren, and they would never have taken something from a family that they couldn't easily cope without.

But that was Gary. Arthur had a different set of motives and right now, his main concern was the RSC driver.

With the dinghy still smouldering in the mud, a long white lorry drove by Kranz's bedroom window. The letters RSC were prominent on the container and Kranz felt better for having glimpsed them in the dark. It was a long way to Scotland, and some HGV drivers preferred the night. The cast and crew for the RSC's Fringe performance would take a few days to catch up with their gear and the container itself was unlikely to be opened before the weekend. By then, Arthur and his men would be poised at the festival.

If Crispin had been aware of any of this, he would have been more than furious, but he wasn't aware of it and in any case, the lodger had stolen his attention. In England, there is a long standing tradition of eating curry after dark and Lucy agreed to indulge.

It was one of Crispin's favourite restaurants and it was a place that completely failed to make an impact on the girl. Lucy had eaten Indian stuff in the States and the set up here was much the same. He wondered if he should have taken her to Ye Old English Hog roast round the corner, but it was too late. Afterwards the waiters left them alone with menus and showed a strange reluctance to return. Crispin glanced from actress to waiting staff and then back to actress again and tried to explain just how flimsy your average Shakespeare biography can be.

"There are all kinds of books about the Bard, but they're mostly nonsense. The writers don't have any hard facts, so they pick out the bits of history they already know and then they try to dress it up like it's something to do with Shakespeare. Your boss in the rehearsal today, he's knocked out a best seller, but it's no more likely to be true than the next one."

Lucy didn't react and Crispin digressed and made the classical error of telling her how pissed off he was with his life. It never works. 'Not for a woman with options. But Crispin did it anyway. Stratford was a very limiting environment to hang out in and he would have preferred to have ended up somewhere with a bit more action.

"So why don't you do that?" she asked, her gaze fixed on the menu.

Crispin was suddenly muddled. "Do what?"

"Leave Stratford."

"*Leave*? What, you mean, just walk away?"

Yes. That's what she meant.

Just walk away.

"Eight weeks ago," she stated, "I was prepping for some big show on Broadway. Then they offered me this thing in Chicago, and then that all went to shit, and then my agent called me and he says, '*Hey*, how about Stratford? So, I said, *sure.* Which Stratford is that?" Lucy snapped her fingers in the air. Actors like to have something physical to do whilst they talk and in the absence of any direction, they tend to invent their own quirks. Tossing the menu to an adjacent table, she moved to adjust her cutlery. "Screw Chicago! Those guys were never going to do it for me anyway."

Crispin didn't comment. Were the people in Chicago never going to do it for her? Or were they a figment of her imagination? He couldn't say.

The food, when it came, was really quite mild and barely a threat to anyone. By the time she asked for coffee, he had already offered to drive her to Scotland. Never averse to a free lunch, Lucy had agreed. They would travel up together in one of the oldest production cars in the world and since there were would only be two seats, there would be no need to argue about passengers.

He stopped. The actress was bored and was able to convey her boredom with a minor twitch of one lip. Time to collect the bill.

Chapter 9

During the summer of 1940, it became clear to the British that the German army was about to attack. Thousands of industrial barges had been assembled in Northern France and a largely improvised invasion fleet was preparing to transport 250,000 men across the Channel. And it was at this point that the officer commanding the British forces reviewed his assets and discovered that for every anti-tank gun facing the beach, there were only three rounds of ammunition. Conscious of the relative inexperience of his men, the officer requested that each gun crew should be allowed to fire one shell into the sea, in order to familiarise themselves with their weapons.

It was not an easy decision. The request ran up the chain of command and by day's end, the cabinet had reached a conclusion: *No*. Better to fire the first of their three shells during the actual attack, on the off chance that one of them might hit something.

Every man in Churchill's cabinet had served in the Great War and it would be misleading to suggest that any of them lacked combat experience. How Britain had gotten itself in such a hopelessly exposed position remains a matter of ongoing debate. And it was, perhaps, in a similar state of mind that the British people awoke to discover that a priceless national asset had been handed over to a bunch of criminals on a plate.

What struck Crispin hardest about 'The Raid' was its audacity. The gang had arrived in a motorised dinghy and simply climbed through a hole in the wall and grabbed the diaries. Sure, they'd had to clobber an ageing security guard, but he was completely unarmed and didn't look that dangerous anyway. Meanwhile, the sole survivor of the operation was offering little in the way of help. Staff at the local hospital were describing Bainbridge as amnesic, but just about conscious. In truth, it seemed that the entire site had been defended by little more than a blue and white ribbon and a couple of worn out trees.

The remains of the dinghy were discovered immediately and on the breakfast news bulletin, the police sounded confident that they could track down the owners. By mid-afternoon, this claim had been modified. Gary had obtained the dinghy by deception, some time ago, and stored the thing in his attic for at least three years. There would be no easy trace.

Shortly after sunrise, Kranz returned to the dig and put on a show of outrage. The Brits were reasonably sympathetic, but there was a process that had to be followed and Kranz didn't argue with them. Since everybody in Stratford was a suspect, Special Branch decided to apprehend him by the Marquee and seize his overcoat. It wasn't a particularly cold day and Kranz was able to retain his dignity with a loose cotton shirt. The coat – he knew – would be passed on to forensics, who would find nothing.

In popular culture, the month of August is sometimes referred to as *the silly season.* The House of Commons is in recess and the newspapers are always on the lookout for something daft. Overnight, the dead security officer had come to represent a cause celeb. His face was on the front cover of every tabloid in the land and like the soldiers with the last three cannon shells in England, this diminutive figure in blue had become Britain's first and last line of defence.

An appeal for the reinstatement of the death penalty soon followed and in an interesting break from tradition, the loudest voices were coming from the educated elite. People who would never have batted an eyelid at a spate of stabbings on your average council estate were suddenly mortified by the loss of one man in Stratford. That, and anything else that might get them on the box besides a picture of The Bard.

Meanwhile, at 23 The Stables, Crispin's disinformation campaign was gathering pace. A very professional fist knocked at the door and as it opened, a flange of rowdy journalists began their chant:

"DOCTOR SHAKESPEARE! DOCTOR SHAKESPEARE!"

Jack's dressing gown had been purchased from a charity shop using old money and was badly in need of an upgrade. Had he expected to appear on every news channel in the English speaking world, he might have worn something else.

"Doctor Shakespeare!"

"Doctor Shakespeare! How do you feel about your great discovery?"

Jack's surprise lasted for about as long as it took him to guess what was happening. This ageing figure in brown was an unlikely candidate for the mythical abseiler from Stratford and in a less frantic state of mind, the people with the microphones might have seen this too.

Twenty minutes down the road, the real abseiler was at ease beneath his duvet. Alone in his Grade III listed cottage, Crispin had spent the morning debating which items to take to with him for Scotland. Driving a wildly impractical vehicle like a Morgan forces a man to make compromises. There was no point in going up there if he didn't take the costumes and if he did take the costumes, he might not be able to fit his lodger in the passenger seat. It was the sort of problem that might have vexed him for longer, but as fate might have it, his old friend Duncan turned up on his doorstep and asked for a cup of tea.

Duncan asked about Jack. Had Crispin heard anything from him yet? Jack was unlikely to contact him by text, but he might well call by in person and it would probably be best to have left the house – or indeed England - before that moment came.

"You know the definition of an alcoholic?" asked Duncan, who was heading into sensitive territory.

Crispin feigned ignorance and Duncan reminded him of a favourite line from their youth.

"Someone who drinks more than his doctor."

That was an old one indeed. Older than their white coats and tacky red stethoscopes. Crispin reckoned it dated back to the middle part of their second year, although neither man was certain. There might have been a case for trying to incorporate it into Duncan's stand-up routine, but it was too late for any major edits, so they boiled the kettle and Duncan talked about the heist. A white transit van had been seen heading to Liverpool on the night of the robbery and the police were searching the docks.

"How do they know it's the same one?" asked Crispin. "There are a lot of white vans on the roads."

The van had been identified from the tyre tracks, down by the canal. Duncan had just read about it on the internet. He talked about the media scrum outside Jack's house and suggested that Crispin take advantage of the situation by selling his story to the press.

"And they'd probably give you a fair whack!" he added. "I mean, how much did you pay for that Morgan?"

This was a rhetorical question and Crispin declined to reply. In any case, the two men had a similar mindset and didn't always need to communicate in words. Like Crispin, Duncan had once dreamt of some ego driven career in a London teaching hospital, and like Crispin he had found himself strangely overlooked by the culture therein. Later – years later - the two of them had drifted back to the West Midlands, where they pretended not to care. Meanwhile, back in the big city, their professors of old were still trapped in the same teaching hospital, surrounded by their eager subordinates, all of them shorter, balder and more boring than themselves. In the crazy, mixed up world of clinical medicine, this sort of thing can feel like defeat. What's more, Crispin's position in a family practice seemed even less prestigious than that of Duncan, who had at least been able to stay in hospital medicine. But that didn't matter. Maybe, Duncan mused, they could find a third shared identity. 'In the world of The Fringe.

Then, without fanfare, Crispin's lodger arrived in the kitchen and all conversation came to an end. Watching her open the fridge, Duncan tried to make contact.

"Morning."

The actress looked for milk and Duncan tried again.

"It's a sort of greeting."

But there was something else going on here, something much more subtle. Duncan wasn't a regular attendee in the Crispin residence and he'd never have driven here just to update him on the news.

In fact, Duncan had come here purely to gather intel on Lucy and he'd be divulging it all, as soon as he left the building. Living with a high profile female came with a price tag and before Crispin could stop her, Lucy had handed over their entire strategy. Her role in the RSC play, her intention to travel up in Crispin's Morgan, the whole shebang. Duncan nodded with a smile of smug satisfaction and Crispin decided to follow him as far as the door.

Chapter 10

The Scottish capital is a hidden gem. In the eyes of many, it can hold its own against Venice, and when seen besides London, it feels raw and untouched. Like Bruges, Prague and Florence, Edinburgh serves to remind us of just how beautiful so many European cities might have been, had the madness of aerial bombing not intervened.

Despite all this, there are people in Scotland with a pretty ambivalent view of the place. In the Highlands, Edinburgh is sometimes described as an English city, with a seat of government that seems at least as distant as Westminster. Lacking the extreme wealth of the British capital, Edinburgh has failed to erase its industrial past and its trademark sandstone remains as dour and as dark as ever.

During the late 20th Century, the city sought to reinvent itself, as a centre for the arts and to the surprise of many, it actually worked. Each and every summer, Edinburgh succumbs to a fringe comedy festival and the streets are briefly transformed. Crispin had been coming here since his earliest days as a medical student and in the whole of that time, the only thing that had really changed was his means of transport.

In his penny-less youth, he used to take the train. Now, he used the car. His Morgan was a romantic but impractical means of travel that consciously harked back to a bygone age. Fun in the sun, it could easily embarrass a man on a wet day, and on this occasion, the wet kicked in around Derby.

Pulling up the hood, Crispin fought to suppress his greatest fear, that fear being that the actress sitting next to him might bore of his company and ask him to drop her off at the nearest railway station. He needn't have worried. Lucy's legs were much shorter than his own and she barely moaned at all.

Besides, the journey itself was not without merit. All of England's countryside was here for the taking and they were still some distance from Scotland. Just after midday, he drove to a forgotten hill top market town where the concept of bling and brand labels had yet to arrive. If they'd been anything less than a hundred miles from London, the entire town centre would have been overrun by tourists. But they weren't near London. They were too far out to feel it and Crispin would have been loath to change a single stone in this street.

Somewhere near the central square there was an elevated bandstand, Roman in its supportive pillars and largely unused in modern times. Having said that, they had discovered the pavement café. The accents were thick, but the service more than made up for it and like a lot of young women, Lucy responded well to a glass of white wine.

Lunch ended and they drifted back to the A1. Just north of the River Tyne, that same road becomes a narrow, winding corridor that makes a man afraid to take his foot off the brake. Rich farm land turns to scraggy moor and the population density falls to nothing.

In time, the heather begins to fade and an astonishing new city takes its place, proclaiming its role in the festival at the very first billboard. Crispin spotted a poster for the RSC performance and moved to nudge Lucy, who was pretending to have not noticed. It was a good, striking piece of work, where Lucy's blurred and fabled torso served as a back drop to the central male characters. His passenger was jubilant and Crispin was pleased for her, though perhaps very slightly confused. Having wallowed in the crass, amateur side of the Festival for so long, he sometimes struggled to understand why a reputable organisation like the RSC would bother to come here. And yet they had, albeit with just the one play:

JULIUS CAESAR, AN RSC PRODUCTION

There are very few places in this world that live up to expectations, but The Royal Mile in Edinburgh is one of them. Lucy thought this city was wonderful, as he had always known she would. With the dual carriage way far behind them, the Morgan approached a run of cobbles and Crispin cut his speed until the cobbles ended and a road of modern asphalt led them down to her hotel.

This was it. Crispin ran around the back of the car and released her suitcase. Like the rest of the luggage, he had strapped it to the boot in a hurry and hoped to hell it was water proof. It was, and the actress broke into a fresh and knowing smile, kissing him very publicly and for much longer than the moment required. Crispin would be staying half a mile down the road and he took the opportunity to remind her of that.

And then she was gone. It might have looked chivalrous to offer to carry her bags but he guessed, correctly, that she would have said no. Standing by the car, he watched her traverse the revolving doors and disappear therein.

She was gone. 'Time to get going.

Chapter 11

Somewhere between graduation and his return to Stratford, Crispin had lost the ability to sleep on the floor and at the Edinburgh Fringe Festival, there are those who would see this as a bad sign. If you can afford your own bedroom, and you aren't fighting over the same bit of rug, you're probably too old for The Fringe.

With his bags unpacked and a clean shirt buttoned, Crispin dashed to the first event on offer and lived to regret it. A Red Brick University review team were doing their best to sound trendy and doing it badly. In fact, they were dreadful. Ten minutes into the performance, he started to wonder whether he should visit the dressing room and tell them all to go home. Too British to actually do anything, he just sat there 'til the curtain fell and it was time to escape.

The doctor fastened his coat and marched through the streets outside.

What about his own writing? Would it fair any better than the crap he'd just seen? And if it did, did it really matter? If he knew what shame was, he wouldn't have come here in the first place. There were thousands of acts at the festival and in itself, a Fringe performance wasn't worth very much at all. But he had to keep going. Edinburgh was the last best hope of every wannabe on the planet and when a man gave up on The Fringe, he was giving up on life itself.

He remembered the story of the comic, John Cleese, and the curious BBC talent scouts who first approached him at this very event. Cleese had just come off stage, the scouts liked what he'd said and the way he said it. The rest is history.

So, the Fringe can work – he told himself – even for the real beginners of this world.

Crispin walked a little further and stumbled across that long white lorry that seemed to be stalking him across the country. There were quite a few of these things in Stratford and it was hard to know if this was the exact same vehicle he had passed on the morning of his infamous visit to the sinkhole. To Crispin, it was little more than a freeze-dried stage show in a box and in the next few days, the RSC people would use its contents to deliver a product of real quality. As far as the *people* bit went, Crispin knew that the rest of the cast would be flying up from Birmingham in the morning. Absent from that flight would be Gordon, the assistant director, who had been here for nearly a week now, and whom Crispin was about to discover in this very street.

"Christ!" gasped the doctor, who recognised the guy from his Saturday morning call out. Draped in a plastic anorak from the late 1970s, Gordon cut a striking figure in green.

"Have you heard?" demanded the assistant director. Crispin hadn't and Gordon decided to tell him. "They found the getaway vehicle in Liverpool."

"Liverpool?"

"Yes. It's all over the news," said Gordon. "The crooks set fire to their van by the docks. No fingerprints, you see. None of that *DNA* stuff. MI5 are still searching the container ships, but they haven't found anything yet."

"MI5?" asked Crispin, visibly shocked. "Surely, that's a job for the police. How do you know it was MI5?"

Gordon didn't. He had made that bit up for additional impact and was visibly shocked that Crispin had rumbled him so quickly.

"But there's definitely no DNA!" he said, sounding a bit more defiant. "Because they said *that* on the television."

Doubtless his other ideas were bonkers too, but Gordon hadn't finished yet. The economy of an entire region had been salvaged by two blokes in black balaclava helmets and there was a widespread sense of anxiety that the wider community might never be able to thank them enough. In an attempt to fill the emotional vacuum, the Bishop of Stratford had arranged a service of thanksgiving in the Church of the Holy Trinity and they were expecting a healthy turnout.

"They've put in a big order for patio furniture, just to spruce up the graveyard," said Gordon. "There won't be enough space in the pews, you see. They've got committed atheists fighting to get in!"

Gordon wanted to keep going, but Crispin decided to deny him the pleasure. Turning his back on the assistant director, he resumed his journey up the hill, finally reaching the shambolic little venue he had hired for his own actors. In an effort to control costs, the Linguists would be sharing with the same Hungarian Lesbian Dancing Troupe they had worked with last year and within seconds of his arrival, Crispin was thrilled to see Duncan, hanging a banner over the door.

Learning By Humiliation.

Down on the pavement, someone asked what it meant and Duncan tried his hand at *helpful*.

"Everything you ever wanted to know about medical school but were afraid to ask." He said.

The man on the pavement was unimpressed. Television had already done this sort of thing to death, and television – he seemed keen to remind them – was free at the point of access.

A little further along the cobbles, the rest of The Linguists were canvassing in full costume with Harry playing himself in a billowing white coat. Six feet to his left, Sarah was standing there in full makeup and a nurse's outfit.

It didn't suit her. Ordinarily, Sarah was very much a straight laced person, forgetful – even now – of those rare moments of digression she had displayed as a medical student. Sarah's latter-day brush with the grown-up world of medicine had merely widened the gap between herself and her slightly zany on stage persona and if he was looking for acting skills, then this was it. Pressing her flyers to a passerby, Sarah did her best to gain attention.

"Here you are, Sir," she said, very politely, "the Cunning Linguists. For five nights only."

Five nights was about as much as they could afford, but Sarah decided not to mention this. In any case, the man in the street was more concerned with semantics.

"The cunning *what*?" They heard him ask. "Is that rude?"

Sarah tried to convince him that it wasn't, but the man was a born sceptic. Much worse than that, he didn't buy a ticket. Glancing through the whole scene, Crispin looked at Harry and thought he saw something else. Somehow, Harry had begun to remind him of a character in an Enid Blyton novel. Not any particular Enid Blyton novel, all of them. The only real distinction was that Harry was entirely post pubertal and knew how to do smut.

Sarah turned to Crispin and decided to deliver the bad news. "There's a burnt out van in Liverpool."

Holding it all together, Crispin did his best to ignore her bright red lipstick and blow up breasts. Definitely not very Enid. Sarah reached out and touched him, but Crispin stepped away from her, saying only, "I know."

Chapter 12

That isn't to say *The Linguists* lacked gusto. Indeed, their poster (singular) campaign was really well phrased:

THE CUNNING LINGUISTS PRESENT...

AN ENTIRELY NEW SHAKESPEAREAN PRODUCTION

LEARNING BY HUMILIATION!

The Hungarians were going on ahead of them and by the time they were done, Crispin's troupe would have less than an hour to reposition the props. Standing tall on a very low cost chair, Harry held up his smart phone and snatched a quick photograph. In days gone by, The Stratford Upon Avon Herald had published this kind of material quite readily, and with Crispin's new status in the town, Harry was expecting the front page.

But not everybody in Scotland was here for their art. Unbeknown to The Linguists and less than a mile down the road, a strange and disparate group of criminals had assembled in a roof top apartment. Leading from the front, Arthur Kranz had clad himself in some unremarkable, nondescript outfit and forgotten to comb his hair. His battered leather suitcase had been flung open on the bed and a well-thumbed copy of *The Complete Works* was out there on the sheets. An inch or two from this hefty little volume lay a photograph of Kranz and his estranged lover, Lucy. Even at this late stage, Kranz liked to carry something with him. Lest he forgot.

Cigarettes were explicitly banned by their landlord, but his crew had been here for some time and the air was thick with smoke. Given the sheer malfeasance of their enterprise, ignoring the ban on cigarettes felt like a particularly minor offence and nobody bothered to stop. The main culprit was Winston, but many a man has found solace in the filter tips and as the day progressed, it became obvious that Gary had some serious issues too.

Alone by the windows, Kranz reviewed the situation in his head.

The documents had been stolen from the British authorities and placed in the RSC lorry. Kranz had left the scene of the crime as if empty handed and gone on to express his outrage to the local press. Meanwhile, the police had scoured every vessel in the port of Liverpool and found a couple of dozen Somalians in a container marked "Frankfurt". It was only a matter of time before his own name came up and Kranz was under considerable pressure to leave these islands soon.

Soon, but not yet. There was treasure to be had here and he was loath to leave without it. More than that, he had a plan to steal it back.

Like most modern logistics groups, the RSC transport department was run on computers and for his tech savvy friends in New York, a quick hack through an English arts charity had been easy money. Kranz had known exactly where this truck was going, long before he boarded his plane at JFK.

By this time tomorrow, the vehicle would be moved to a new position, some distance from the theatre and much closer to a nearby park. Then, just after midnight, Kranz's team would go in hard. The first of those men was a heavily built bruiser from East London. At six feet two, Winston was a head taller than Arthur and looked like a surefire winner in any kind of scrap. Winston had made the effort to wear his blue baseball cap the right way round.

The second man, Al, had trailed Kranz across the Atlantic and was a regular member of his team. Many years ago, Al had adopted the habit of swinging his baseball cap in a reversed position and in the course of time it had become the feature that seemed to define him.

The third and final figure of Gary, was a second native of the British Isles. Ten years younger than Al with a head of radiant red hair, Gary had been and born and bred in the northeast of England and spoke with a rhythm and a dialect all of his own.

Over by the door, Al read from a National newspaper: GUARD SUCCUMBS TO WOUNDS.

The article was accompanied by a blurred picture of a decidedly *ex*-security guard. Sensing that Al had a problem with complex narrative, Winston dragged the thing away from him and started to read out loud: "The search for the Stratford Documents has become a murder inquiry following the death of a museum employee. Scotland Yard are preparing a photo-fit of the likely assailant."

The rest of the room fell silent and Al felt the need to comment, "Hey, Kranz, ain't that something? They still call it *Scotland Yard*. Like that Sherlock Holmes. Can you believe it?"

Kranz could believe it, but Gary's mind was moving on.

"*Murder!* Nobody gives a damn about the shit they dig up. But if you've duffed some cock in a blue jacket, they'll never let it go."

Winston recalled the Great Train Robbery and the ultimate fate of a man called Briggs. It was a reference that drew a blank from Al, but saw Gary grimace in his own corner.

Over by the window, their esteemed leader was still in control.

"Great men…" he mumbled, "…must great burdens bear."

Resting the binoculars on the desk, Arthur Kranz returned to his tablet and swept one finger across the screen. First colour, then black and white images jumped up in his face and then suddenly, in the darkened streets of Stratford, he saw a lorry.

Kranz spread his fingers and watched, enthralled, as the vehicle expanded and the number plate came into view.

Discarding his tablet, he returned to the binoculars. Distant in the streets beneath him, this exact same vehicle was parked outside the RSC theatre today.

Over on the sofa, Al's chest was seizing up. It might have been the smoke, but both of his lungs had seen better days and Al had long wrestled with his tough guy image. Reaching for his inhaler again, Al sucked greedily on a blue plastic tube. Seconds later, the tension eased and everyone heard him cough.

Alone besides the window, Arthur was back with his tablet where he had managed to find a second image of his former lover from the States. She was sitting in a handmade English sports car, all smiles on her way to Scotland. Crispin's smartphone had been a second, easy hack for his friends in Manhattan and Arthur had downloaded the entire album overnight.

"That girl came too," said Al, his voice hoarse as the ventolin kicked in. "In that fancy car."

"And the books are still in the truck," said Arthur. "What do you think brought me to these God forsaken islands in the first place?"

"I'm not sure," called Winston. "Do you think he's getting anywhere?"

A wave of blue collar laughter rolled out across the attic and Arthur Kranz felt an urge to walk over to Winston and punch him in the face. Either that or go somewhere else. Too proud to actually get up, he sat there a full fifteen minutes before reaching for his coat. A short while later, he was down on the cobbles and sifting through the street ads, eager to distract himself with some low grade fun.

In that sense, he was spoilt for choice. Each and every day, there are hundreds of low grade acts at The Fringe. Barely any of them have a budget to speak of, but there's never a shortage of posters and flyers on this or any other street. Even in a crowded field, one particular act stood out in his mind and the American decided to demean himself further by actually buying a ticket for the thing and taking a seat on the back row. In so far as he had any expectations at all, it was of a down market and entirely British affair. He was wrong. The American influence on Crispin's work was alive and well and had been carefully crafted to drive Kranz to distraction. Within seconds of the opening sequence, the same pointless little bastard who had discovered the diaries was up there on the stage, dressed in the uniform of an American Air Force Officer. The "*Star Spangled Banner*" blared very loudly on a Ghetto Blaster until Crispin reached the podium and Duncan hit on Stop.

"*God bless America!*"

The crowd – who might well have heard this one before – declined to laugh.

"And if He doesn't, *we'll blow Him up!*"

It was a strong and steady carry through and the crowd was open with its appreciation. But Crispin's presence was merely fleeting and he was quickly replaced by a pack of rowdy kids in white. They were supposed to be doctors, although none of them resembled any of the medics that Kranz had ever seen. Theirs was a homage to a bygone age, where every London teaching hospital was a small, self-contained unit and petty cliques jostled for peer approval.

The show ended in just under 60 minutes and The Linguists lined up for one last round of applause. It wasn't exactly ground breaking, but it was there and when it was done, Arthur Kranz felt a desperate need for air. Huddled and alone in the light drizzle, he strode through blackened sandstone. In a street that had been built for horse drawn carriages, Kranz felt suddenly trapped, as if in a narrow crevice. And yet – even now – even in this torrid, fugue-like state, his mind was racing and his thoughts had progressed to a new and fantastical theme: *Youth*. That ill-defined feature of Crispin's people that left them fresh when they should have been tired, funny when they were merely absurd.

Suddenly, Kranz heard the piercing squeal of a teenage girl. It was a scream that seemed both distant and close, with a powerful sexual subtext. Spinning his head in fear, he glimpsed only darkness. What should he do? Run to save her? Race to pile in? All across this city, freshman types were shrieking without reason and Kranz felt the urge to discard the shackles of the adult world and join them by the bar.

He couldn't. He was too far gone. From the moment he punched that guard in Stratford, he had set out on a journey of no return. Possession of the documents would represent an epiphany in his life as a collector, but every achievement comes with a price tag and when this thing was over, there might not be anyone left around him to share it with.

Whilst Kranz fretted, his former girlfriend, Lucy, was fighting to carve her own niche. In modern times, it has become fashionable to criticise the Roman Play for the scarcity of female roles. Given that Shakespeare never actually employed any women, it's hard to imagine his own troupe were particularly bothered by this one, and as far as *Julius Caesar* goes, being his wife is about as good as it gets.

But Caesar's relationship with his wife is an oddity, to say the least. Somewhere in the First Act, he actually turns to Mark Anthony and invites him to bed his own spouse. With Calpurnia in the family way, public opinion might be swayed in Caesar's favour and the world at large might come to see him as a much younger, virile figure than he really is. Statesmen who beg a friend to bed their own wife aren't particularly thick on the ground in English Literature, but Shakespeare does it anyway.

Sensing that Caesar's trip to the Senate might be his last, Calpurnia tries her damnedest to hold the guy back. Crispin, who had arrived late for this performance, caught the scene in its entirety and for Crispin, the most obvious resonance here was with Macbeth, where the title figure baulks openly at the scale of his challenge and it is Lady Macbeth that goads him on. In the Roman Play, the roles are reversed and it is the wife who preaches caution. But caution doesn't come easily to Caesar and pride will be his downfall, driving him on to his own destruction.

The play ended and the crowd rose in appreciation. Here was a cast that knew how to take an encore and when it was over, Crispin left with the crowd, wandering through to an open air bar and grabbing himself a beer.

Several theatres had spilled out into this same area and the place was packed with revellers. Conversation was very loud, but Crispin wanted no part of it. Instead, he felt an aching desire to run round the back and offer his congratulations to Lucy, but guessed, correctly, that there would be people already in there. Lucy's performance had been the standout event in an otherwise weak production and it had not gone unnoticed. The same men who had so often taunted her through rehearsal were fighting to get in close and stroke her butt. Such is the way of things, the way of the theatre.

And what about the Bard? Would he have anything good to say about *this*, rather than any of the other Calpurnias that had ever trod these boards?

It's hard to say.

In truth, Shakespeare is both a familiar and a distant figure whose opinion we often struggle to infer. Starved of any real data, most of his biographers stare out at the backdrop to his life and search for some petty anecdote. And why not? Surely – Crispin reasoned – Chekov was talking rubbish. Surely, the life and times of any writer will always affect their work?

Feeling for his smart phone, Crispin searched on the play.

Although Julius Caesar appears in the First Folio, in 1623, an individual performance of the play is mentioned in the diary of Thomas Platter the younger, in 1599. The play is, however, absent from the list of Shakespearean plays published by Francis Meres in 1598 and, by implication, was probably written in 1599. If this is true, then Julius Caesar has one of the most precise datings of any Shakespearean play. In addition, the style and metre of the work is similar to Henry V, Hamlet and As You Like It, which would further strengthen the conviction that 1599 was the year of first performance.

As Crispin saw it, this was all speculation and if the diaries of William Shakespeare became public knowledge, then a completely different sequence of events might soon emerge.

"Hey mate?"

A new voice was talking to him.

Crispin looked up and saw a tall, lean man with dodgy facial hair and a spray tan face. For a few seconds, his mind was blank, then he got it: this guy was a *Hungarian.*

"Oh, right!" laughed Crispin, reaching out and shaking a spray tan hand. "How's it going?"

"Oh, not too bad." The Hungarian glanced across the square and nodded to some other numskull with a similar beard. "I'm having a bit of friction with me old colleagues though." Crispin looked more carefully. The other bearded guy was a little shorter and about twenty feet away. Conscious that he was under discussion, the second guy refused to return their gaze. Ordinarily, Crispin only helped these people on and off the stage, but in the circumstances he was willing to speak to anybody.

"What is it?" asked Crispin, trying to sound helpful. "Creative differences?"

"Well, he's a new one. We didn't have him last year. But we had this bloke drop out and I like to keep it at a full eight. Back in Croydon, he managed to convince me he could do it, but now we've seen him on stage." Bearded guy rolled his eyes and shook his head in frank despair. "He thinks he's got it, but he's just not a Hungarian lesbian! And I've had to tell him that. Even if he is a Hungarian, he can't bloody dance! You know what I mean?"

Crispin nodded with real sympathy and did his best to sound supportive, adding,

"Well, you've got to protect your brand."

"And I've got to protect my troupe! You should see us in Croydon. We've got a real presence."

His counterpart nodded back ferociously and turned to some other bloke with a bit of a beard and a South London accent who Crispin recognised from last year. "Too bloody right." mumbled third Hungarian.

The Hungarians were having problems, that much was certain, but Crispin couldn't help them. Instead, he downed his first pint and crushed the clear plastic glass in one hand. It was a slow and intricate process that consumed most of his brain cells for the best part of five minutes and when he had finished and the glass was destroyed, he looked to Lucy's dressing room, and saw that she had yet to emerge.

It was time to get going.

Heading home along the High Street, Crispin tried to imagine a life where a woman might receive a better offer, every time she back tracked to her own dressing room. Where there were men on standby to stroke her butt, just because of her performance on stage. He couldn't, it was a world so far removed from his own that he could never know how it felt.

He thought about Sarah and the very slightly cold and soulless building where they were paying her to practice medicine. Someday soon, Jack would retire from the business and Crispin had been earmarked to take command. Things that had seemed impossible in the recent past might suddenly become straightforward. Maybe, he should offer Sarah a position in his own clinic. He'd have to place a formal advertisement in the medical press, but lots of people did that, even when they'd already decided who they were going to give it to. Alone in the half light, he remembered the first time he had set eyes on that girl. Sarah had been wrapped in clear plastic and baffled by the sequence of tendons in a cadaveric hand. Even now – ten years down the line – he could still smell the formalin. It was one of the most fateful meetings of his life and one that he would never experience again. Smiling in the course of his homeward march, Crispin recalled those days with real affection.

It was dark now and he was tired. Maybe he had tried to do too much. He had a habit of trying to do too much and it was a habit he needed to kick. Stumbling through the hotel lobby, he took hold of the bannister and used it to haul himself up. One step short of the finish line, a digital lock seemed hell bent on blocking his journey and just before he tried to head butt the door, a red light faded and a green one burst into life. Seconds later, he was surprised to find an American actress on his bed sheets, resplendent in Gap casuals with hair and make up from the RSC.

How the hell had she gotten here before him? More to the point, how had she gotten past the reception desk and the electronic lock?

He glanced at the window and tried to convince himself that it was much too small for her to climb through. As far as he knew there were no trap doors and no secret hatches. And yet she was here and she was starting to undress. There are a lot of ways for a woman to take her clothes off and some of them can seem forced, giddy or even contrived. But with Lucy, Crispin saw something different: *disinterest.* A world weary feel for the act of disrobement that was as much unsettling as it was fun.

Outside and on the pavement, Lucy's decidedly *ex-*boyfriend could see nothing, but sensed much. Having followed her this far, Arthur Kranz had expected that Lucy would lead him back to her hotel. Instead, she had drifted somewhere else. Somewhere new. To say that he resented this decision would have been an understatement, but this is where they were and Arthur had long acknowledged that Lucy had a life and a mind of her own.

He remembered her as they'd first met: blonder, younger and even thinner than she had been tonight. Less than two years had elapsed since that day, but deep down, Arthur's mind had aged another ten.

There are many thresholds we have to cross in this life, and for the modern woman, one of them is the open door of an older man's car. Kranz had made the appropriate gesture and Lucy hadn't let him down. As he remembered it, he had known her for less than fifteen minutes. He drove them both to some bar he knew, well out of town and clear from the prying gaze of his all-seeing, all knowing friends. There was an age gap, sure, and it seemed likely that the people in the bar thought less of him because of it, but Kranz didn't care about the people in the bar. He cared about himself. He cared about some ill defined barometer of onboard happiness that was swirling, sharply to the right. At that stage, she was playing dumb, going wide eyed with his passing wisecracks. Later, she seemed to sit there and marvel at the sheer scale and grandiosity of his achievements. But that was what he had wanted her to say and Kranz could see something else. A woman who had actually played those same human visions that Kranz had only thought about, admittedly in all the chicken-shit, low profile venues of this world.

Had the University fully appreciated their relationship, then Kranz's position there might have been compromised. But what was that? Hadn't he already risked his very freedom, a hundred times in the course of his life? Collecting those historic artefacts that meant so little to the average guy and so much to himself.

Where was the point in her paying her own rent? They would leave every morning in separate cars and maintain the illusion of unconnected lives. It was pragmatic. He was saving her money and as he awoke, again and again with his skin bathed in her hair, there was a cumulative ache and a summated passion that had prompted him to demand marriage and thus the reassurance that she would always be there. She said no. Worse than that, she laughed at him and he threw her out, guessing, correctly, that she had a life and a game plan of her own.

So it was over. A thing from his past. 'Time to move on.

Alone in a sandstone street, Arthur pulled out his smartphone and did a quick Google search on Crispin's name. It might have been more sensible to do this in the attic, but he had failed to anticipate how long and how totally this kid would impinge upon his life.

The search engines fired and Kranz began to scroll. Crispin wasn't famous, but he had collected a reasonable number of hits. His qualification as a doctor had been reported in the local press and there was a lengthy string of headlines about his antics at The Fringe. Next came the day of his appointment to the family practice in Stratford, then the explosion of material surrounding the documents.

Fifty feet above the road, Crispin wasn't using a search engine. His thoughts were firmly in the present and he had just discovered a side to his lodger that had previously passed him by.

Purposely underfed since her early twenties, she seemed to fuse the brutal lines of an anatomical specimen with the fashionable aesthetics of her time. And yet, for all her near emaciation, there was a verve and a physical energy he might not have expected.

She ensnared him – effortlessly – from a supine position and revelled silently in the wake of his mouth. Somewhere in the mid-distance, a car back-fired. Neither party reacted. The world outside was another time zone and Crispin saw no link between the two. Eventually this bed and the room and the world fell silent, and he lay there, and listened without comment whilst she regressed to her childhood and spoke to him, softly about the role of drugs.

"You know" – he heard her breathe – "most of the time I was on *coke*. I was lucky to get out of it, really. I got out before they took my doe."

In his day job, lots of people lied to him and their motive – in so far as they had a motive – was usually cash. Whilst his career was young, Crispin had developed an ability to spot them straight away. But Lucy was different. Lucy was an actress and she played with people's emotions for a living. Was this particular sob story real?

Or were these the pages of some forgotten manuscript? He couldn't say.

"What's it like?"

For an instant, he felt like some hapless extra in an Eric Idle sketch. Was he supposed to have snorted this stuff himself? As part of a broad and liberal education? He couldn't say.

"Oh, coke's wonderful," she groaned, her spine arching with the thought in her veins.

Sexual contact, she told him, was easy for girls and sexual pleasure had been intertwined with the rich tapestry of her life in much the same way as books and learning had been woven into his. Algebra was an anathema to her, as was the ultra-structure of the cell. Everything that had given succour to Crispin's childhood had been sidelined in her own. And yet, somehow, Lucy had survived and prospered, finding a home on the English stage. His main concern for her today was that she wouldn't be able to cope with the thing they call ageing, and he knew that in the world of the theatre, she would find little or no financial security. But Lucy wasn't troubled by these things. Thus far, her body had carried her through. In the faded mirror of a public convenience, it had silenced her peers and emboldened her soul. It was her rod and her staff. It comforted her in dark places and she had yet to arrive at a brief or a party where her face had been ignored and the cocktails had come with a bill. Life itself was an all immersive experience for Lucy, and she had no insight into such everyday foibles as pain, rejection or fear.

They dozed off again and then he awoke on the bed sheets, strangely shaken by the act of love. For some reason, he stared at the curtains for the best part of thirty seconds.

He remembered the mother of whom he had so often dreamt and tried to recall his fantastic grief on the day she had disappeared. He could not. Someone very clever had right clicked on that entire icon and dragged it down into *trash*. Now – perhaps for the first time – he sensed a perverse pleasure in her leaving because no matter what happened next, he would never have to say sorry to his parents. Only to Jack. Here, on a damp mattress at The Fringe, he could lie by a lunatic and feel no guilt.

The doctor sighed and blacked out for a while and then he awoke with the sun and pulled himself free of the sheets.

She was gone. She had left him in the night and taken what physical possessions she had with her. In Crispin's mind, it was not inconceivable that he had imagined the whole thing. Rolling back across the mattress, he searched for evidence and found a streak of makeup on one pillow. It was the only sign she had ever been here and Crispin began to wonder if her name was really *Lucy* at all.

Chapter 13

He stole some more sleep and rose at a sensible hour. And then he left the hotel and trotted over to his cast. They were loud and unready, but it was time to get going and so the entire pack of them staggered down towards the theatre and slithered into their low cost, homemade costumes. Numbers were up on the previous day, but they were unlikely to recover their costs.

As per normal, their opening scene was over very quickly and within seconds, they had switched to a musical number. If nothing else, *The Linguists* had mastered the art of rapid turnaround and before the audience had time to recover from the first gag, they were onto the next.

Stage left came a young woman, arm in arm with her doting boyfriend. Seconds later they were approached by an ageing figure in a long white coat.

"Now then, young man. What manner of work are you in?"

"I'm your house officer, Doctor Smith."

To his credit, Duncan did *surprise*, very well. Better than that, he could even do *old*.

"Good Lord!"

Crispin, who had watched Duncan before, broke into a smile. It was hardly random. Every so often, a guy on The Fringe makes the leap from amateur to professional and if there was one man amongst them who might straddle that gap, then it was Duncan.

This scene had a habit of dragging on and in the course of rehearsal, Crispin had decided to cut it down. Exit Sarah, stage left, pursued by an endoscopist. Their timing was spot on and the crowd was crying for more.

Turning his thoughts to that crowd, Crispin saw a familiar face at the rear of the room.

To be sitting there at all, she must have purchased a ticket, but he couldn't be certain she would stay. He felt an impulse to storm over to the back row and ask her how she'd broken into his room and why the hell she'd vanished in the night, but his people were still on stage and it wasn't the right moment. As soon as the show ended, he caught up with her again, blocking the exit in person and waiting for her to come through.

What did she think to it?

To what? The play? The play was good. 'Better than she had expected. She would like to have stayed and watched the matinee performance too, but they were already texting her from the RSC. She said something about catching up later and brushed past him on her way to the door.

Most probably, he realised, she thought it was crap.

With the public expelled, the Hungarian Lesbian Dancing Troupe appeared out of no-where and started to roam their collective stage. Two hours later, the Linguists came back for more and then, as the sky darkened, Crispin felt the heavy hand of Duncan press down upon his shoulder.

"C'mon," said the endoscopist, "let's go." Or words to that extent and they kicked away the wreckage and marched to the pub as a group. The pub wasn't that great either, but the Fringe was a special place for The Linguists and there were rituals they were obliged to perform. Sarah bought Crispin a pint and the rest of them stood around and watched whilst he downed the thing in one. In days gone by, he could have done it at the drop of a hat. Tonight, he actually broke off to belch and rest his jaw. Bits of it came streaming down his face, but they decided not to count that and his followers were satisfied.

He could still hack it. The gap between where they were now and their once zany lives as medical students was still a brief one, and his glass was empty and standing there on the bar. Turning to his cast, Crispin looked for signs of dissent.

None were forthcoming.

It felt better. It felt like some massive burden had been lifted from his shoulders and discarded in the street. The rebellion that had threatened to destroy him in Stratford had petered out. In fact, everything was looking a bit rosier to Crispin, right up until the point when the man behind the bar fiddled with the plasma screen and an unnamed journalist called out from above.

"Excitement surrounding the find has faded, following the release of new scientific data."

The journalist vanished and a stout man in a raincoat moved to take her place. Chief Inspector Higgins had been enshrined by a sea of black microphones and he spoke using a small white card as a prompt.

"Carbon fourteen dating," he announced, "confirms that the missing documents were manufactured in the eighteenth century."

Off camera, a voice from the scrum asked a new question. "So that would make an Elizabethan find unlikely?"

"Is that a question or a statement?"

Comic timing isn't a job requirement for the West Midlands Constabulary and Higgins failed to get a laugh. Nevertheless, he did make an effort to press his point home.

"I think we can forget that one now. My understanding is that the British Museum will be scaling back their operation here, very shortly."

Back in Scotland, the not so Cunning Linguists were suddenly tight-lipped. Drinking a pint and a half of lager very quickly was as good a way as any to ease a man's pain, but after this broadcast, it might not be enough.

"There you go!" said the barman. "All that fuss and nothing to show for it. They can't even catch a bleedin' book thief!"

"How about Lucy?" asked Harry, pursuing a different line. "Have you made any progress there?" Something in Crispin's face seemed to say that he hadn't. "Well, as your psychoanalyst, I'd strongly recommend that you do. You might feel like shit today, but there are a lot of endorphins in your head, just waiting to break out and there's only one way to set them free. In any case, what else have you got to do all day?"

"I see a lot of kiddies with earache."

Before Harry could react to this one, the aforementioned actress returned to their lives in person.

"Lucy baby! Have you met Crispin? Very talented man. Blues for Cambridge!" And this was not, Harry added, a mood state. "That's blues for sword fencing."

But Crispin wasn't interested in sword fencing. His mind was still on the news.

"It's the wrong sort of carbon," he told her.

"In the books?" asked Lucy. Crispin nodded and the actress shrugged without emotion. "Aw, so what? What were you hoping for? *Bill's Diaries*?"

Lucy had stirred something up and Crispin took it badly.

"You don't need to read a man's diary to know what makes him tick," he insisted. "When a guy pours his soul onto the page, that's when you'll hear the truth. Fiction tells it all."

"You're sure?"

"Of course. Nobody can hide it. Not when they're writing."

Crispin had been beaten. His miraculous breakthrough for English literature was little more than a glitch in the online news. Slowly, much more slowly than he would have liked to, he turned to his lodger and asked if she wanted to eat.

Chapter 14

Crispin and Lucy sat opposite one another in a crowded room.

He tried to explain *Cambridge* and *The Blues* and did his best to say sorry for Harry. "It's difficult with these mental health people." he persisted. "That guy spends all day with mad people and I think it can rub off. Basically, I wasn't in Cambridge at all, although I did have a stab at the old sword fencing."

He tried stabbing the Earth's atmosphere with one finger, just to prove his point, but she wasn't impressed. Instead, she decided to surprise him further by changing the subject.

"Never love an actress. And if you do, only love a bad one."

"A bad actress?"

"Yes," said Lucy. "Anyone can screw you over, but most of them aren't very good at it."

A bad actress, it transpired, was practically normal and normal people were a lot easier to cope with.

"As oppose to a good actress?" asked Crispin, doubling back on her line. "Who isn't easy to read?"

"If they get you at an early age," she told him, "you don't even know you're doing it."

"And did they? Get you early?"

She didn't reply.

He took the bill and they walked outside. Fresh in the night air, the scale and splendour of this city seemed to overwhelm the pair of them and he asked her again about her father.

"Why are you asking me that? You're nuts for these people you're never going to meet."

"You're sure he wasn't a doctor? You're not one of these idiots who keeps looking for men like their father?"

No! Lucy's father was a great many things, all rolled into one. A little Jewish, mostly Swedish, very slightly Welsh. 'All American.

"How about you?"

"When I was a kid," said Crispin, "there were some dreadful rumours about Ireland. Luckily, I was able to play them down. Later on, it turned out we were twenty-five per cent Scottish but I've managed to come to terms with it. Mostly English, I'm afraid."

They paused at the summit of a long and gentle slope and Crispin delivered his summing up speech: "You know, ordinarily, I'm fiercely intolerant of racial and religious differences, but in your case, I'm willing to make an exception."

And then he kissed her, slowly at first and then with real energy. She was lying to him - he knew - but that didn't matter. She was fun and he was two hundred miles from home, alive and well in a Highland breeze. He was laughing, he was smiling. He was fourteen years old for the first time in his life. Edinburgh was fading out and if it wasn't for the strength of the cross wind, they might have stayed there for much longer.

Instead, they moved on, reaching the brow of the hill and then picking up speed on the downwards slope. Like so many historic cities, the magic faded very suddenly on these quiet, peripheral streets, only coming back to greet them as slope ended and a run of park land approached. Leaner and more casually dressed than Crispin, Lucy raced ahead of him, colliding in the process with a taller, stronger man. It was Arthur Kranz himself. A little Jewish, a little Irish, very slightly Swedish. 'All American. Lucy's half-forgotten lover from a near forgotten world.

Lucy gulped, audibly and Arthur felt himself baited by the taste of her breath.

"*Arthur?*"

Arthur's khaki raincoat was grey, and his stunted, checkered hat, a dull blur in the night. His eyes were hidden by heavily mirrored spectacles and his jaw darkened by a full ten days of stubble.

"What are you doing *here*?" asked Lucy, with real shock. "I thought... I thought you were in the States!"

To Bainbridge, Arthur had seemed hesitant. But that was Bainbridge. Arthur had one voice for the world and another for Lucy.

"Not now. Not with you out here all alone."

Having fallen behind, Crispin watched from a distance, a deep groan of recognition emerging in his heart. This sort of thing had happened to him before and when it did, it was usually pretty dreadful.

Lucy had frozen and Crispin was reluctant to catch her up.

"Yes," she blurted. "But what are you *doing*?"

Crispin was about to say something too when his head turned to a long, white lorry, silent in a nearby alley. Prominent at the back of the lorry, a heavily built driver was preparing to light up a cigarette. Seconds later, two sinister figures in black ran from the shadows and moved to attack.

Crispin spat in the obscene and sprinted forward, desperate to make his first rugby tackle in years. Furious in the sidelines, Arthur Kranz glanced over to his left and watched, aghast, as the first of his men went down. It was dark now, Al was facing the driver and Kranz's men were about to disappoint him badly. Worse still, the driver knew how to handle himself much better than anyone could have guessed. Getting in close, Al took a single blow to the stomach and almost fell flat on the spot.

Further afield, a young American actress was elated.

"*Stop!*" screeched Lucy, who wanted nothing of the sort.

There are some noises in the night that people ignore and some that bring them on. Lucy was bringing them on and Arthur held her by the mouth and shouted very loudly, "Don't get involved!"

And so she stayed there, cold and tense in the ferocious grip of an older man. Fifty yards ahead of them, Winston rose up from the tackle and took a fresh swipe at his opponent. Further forward, Al had reached the cabin and wasted no time in his bid to command the vast rear doors. Seconds later, a single wooden box fell out from the back, spilling its contents onto gleaming concrete. To Crispin, it seemed that there were potential weapons here and he snatched a theatrical sword from the floor and lurched instinctively, towards Winston, convinced that his time as a competitive fencer might give him the edge. It didn't. This was a battle without ritual or restraint, but the RSC driver was more than willing to make up for this with sheer brawn. Striding forwards with clenched fists, he punched and whipped his assailants back towards a low stone wall.

Al's next move had been planned in advance. He jumped. Winston followed and suddenly Crispin was alone besides the parapets. Dropping his ridiculous little weapon on the paving stones, he stepped forward and looked out over the edge. What had seemed like a giant leap to nowhere actually ended in soft parkland. Their attackers had identified this route in daylight and decided to take it if anything went amiss.

Walking back to the driver, Crispin tried to make himself useful, asking, "You alright, mate?"

The driver touched his own forehead. "Jesus!"

He had survived. More than that, he had practically beaten the enemy on his own, although he was more than happy to give credit to Crispin. "You let 'im get up," said the driver, offering a brief lesson in the lost art of street fighting. "If yer can get 'em on the floor, yer mun't let them get up. Keep putting your boot in 'till you've got 'em down."

The doctor made a bid to check him over, starting with the brow and the driver took it badly.

"*Get orrfff.*"

And then the driver shuffled to one side and rested by the side of his huge and spacious vehicle, mouthing off about something new.

"What were they gonna to nick in this thing?"

Which was an entirely pertinent question. Going in blind against an RSC lorry was one of the dumbest crimes that Crispin could imagine. Confused besides the rear number plate, he toed a plastic skull and watched it recoil from a massive tyre.

"I don't know," said Crispin, very quietly. "Yorick's skull, I guess."

But if Crispin was doing *confused*, Kranz was going for *livid*. His plan had failed and unwanted attention was fast approaching. His grip weakened and the woman broke free.

"Crispin!" She shouted, running forwards and reaching Crispin by the lorry. Their embrace, when it came, was brief and very clumsy but it was enough to jar what little audience they had. Digging deep in her pockets, Lucy even made a bid to call the authorities, but Crispin snatched the phone away from her hands and did his best to offend her further.

"You think I can't call the cops?"

Evidently, he didn't, because Crispin was performing that very task himself and when Lucy turned towards the pavement, Kranz had vanished.

A short while later, the police were upon them, loud, brash and for the most part, disinterested. In a matter of minutes, they were directing the survivors to A&E. As soon as they arrived, Crispin and the driver were subjected to the obligatory non-event that is the NHS waiting room. Eons into their ordeal, Crispin and his accomplice were shunted into adjacent cubicles until suddenly, some lanky kid in green pyjamas pitched up with a syringe and tried to stab the driver in the head. Apparently, it was time to suture his scalp wound. It was a slow, difficult process that was repeatedly stopped when the driver threatened to kill the attending physician. Reproaching himself with each and every outburst, the driver waited for all the loose ends to be cut before changing tactics and pinning for a sick note. Moments later, one final needle pierced his skin and the cycle began afresh.

Some other doctor arrived and examined Crispin in detail. Apparently, he was going to live after all and a few minutes later, Lucy turned up with a can of full-fat Coke and a copy of the local advertiser.

"What did they want?" Lucy asked, sweeping one hand across his face.

"I don't know," he answered. "'Yorick's skull, I guess."

"Why would they want that?"

Crispin warned her about the raging international black market in Yorick Skulls and the actress denied him the pleasure of a smile, revealing instead the centre pages of her free newspaper.

NEW SHAKESPEAREAN PRODUCTION DRAWS PRAISE.

The column was barely an inch wide and easy to miss, dwarfed as it was, by a plug for a second-hand car dealership on the right.

"Fame at last." she whispered.

"It's the East Caledonian Echo," said Crispin, checking the header. "Who the hell is going to buy the *East Caledonian Echo*?"

"Nobody." Said Lucy. "It's full of adverts. I think you get it for free."

This was a fair point, but it wasn't enough. Crispin had already seen her with Arthur Kranz and wanted an explanation. Pressed a little further, Lucy described the man by the battlements as *a* boyfriend. Singular.

"Soon to become ex?"

But Lucy was non-committal. Within the confines of her own mind, the very ground that they stood on was a stage and Crispin was but an ill-defined figure who played upon it. Somewhere in the background, there was a man with a feathered quill. They'd got him working on the third and Final Act and there was no telling when he'd be done.

"Jesus!"

What – he demanded – had this Kranz character said to her? More to the point, what the hell was this lesser known art historian doing in Scotland?

Things were getting out of hand, but this unlikely looking couple were about to discover a new kind of problem. Matron said they were getting too loud for her cubicles and she wanted them out.

And so they left, willingly and without undue friction, but this was Scotland and the world outside was a much colder, starker place than the one he been waiting for. Dignified on the wet asphalt, Crispin felt a new and unexpected burst of sadness. He had sunk to the level of the people who disrupt an NHS waiting room for a laugh and it didn't make him feel any better.

The two of them made it as far as the taxi ramp, him with a daft dressing on his chin.

"So, when do you leave?"

In the morning. Lucy was leaving for London in the morning.

"For work."

Crispin didn't ask how long, but she decided to tell him anyway: "A month or two."

Less than that if the yield was poor.

He talked about his house and his life in Stratford and tried to remind her of the extremely good time that a man can make on the M40, but she showed no interest. The Fringe, she told him, was something she had already done. In any case, Stratford would still be there in the winter, assuming the little bastards were willing to take her back. And on the basis of her performance in Scotland, she believed that they would.

She stepped away from him, less than an inch or so it seemed, and Crispin made a mental note never to get involved with her again.

"So, who are you really and what were you before? What did you do and why did you do it?"

But Lucy stayed tight lipped. If Crispin had ever thought that he might have had some sort of shared future with this woman, then he was wrong. Most probably, he had known this from the day she had first walked into his house. Whatever, there was no room in his life for grief and if grief came knocking now, he would push it aside. More than that, he would be dismissive.

Chapter 15

Alone again in his hotel room, Crispin kept at it with the dismissive thing. Better than that, he was able to distract himself with another issue. Earlier that same evening, he had given a statement to the police and forgotten to mention Kranz.

Who was the man in the camel raincoat and the checkered hat? And why hadn't Crispin described his presence to the police?

Tearing his soul away from the bed, he sat upright and rubbed one hand against his chin. He should have shaved, several days ago, but Crispin had long struggled with such everyday niceties as shaving. Shaving was something for other people. 'Lesser mortals. The doctor craved a broader canvas.

Years ago – in a hospice – a dying man had offered to give him a lesson in life. There isn't a lot else to do once they take you to a hospice and on this occasion, it was a lesson about the difference between two very similar themes: *love* and *romance*. Romance – Crispin discovered – was a phenomenon that lasts for as long as you are with another person. But love is different. Love goes on, long after that person has disappeared from your life.

At the time and by the bedside, the lesson failed to make much of an impact on him, but it was the sort of thing that can play on your soul in the dark and in the early hours of the morning, Crispin developed a genuine problem with his sleep. There had to be more to this lesson than he had already heard and when the Sun rose, he returned to his patient in haste.

Too late. The bed was empty and a pair of portly women in red were stripping the mattress bare.

That place had been easy money, but his contract there had been a short one and in many ways, Crispin saw this as a good thing. Although he had long been familiar with death, Crispin had never felt comfortable in its presence.

And so, he slept a little more and awoke on a cold, white sheet in Scotland with a sharper, clearer mind. It was gone 10 now and he dressed for the day and rushed down stairs. A few blocks away, his collaborators had hired a three-bedroom flat for the festival. Theirs was a fine, grandiose complex that had never been tempered by such new-fangled pleasures as an elevator.

Breathless with the ascent, Crispin entered the living room and discovered Sarah on a sofa in a pair of dark jeans and a silly nurse's hat. The two didn't go together, but this was the Fringe and as Crispin well knew, nothing goes together in the Fringe. The woman was reading a copy of the East Caledonian Echo, holding the thing up in case he'd missed it. "There you go," she laughed. "It's all happening!"

Sarah removed her hat and Crispin found himself forced to watch as her bronzed and lengthy hair poured down and out across her face. Long hair isn't an easy thing to live with and this kind of hair says as much about a woman's will power as it does her immediate appearance. She reminded him of all the other dreadfully well-healed girls that had trailed him through medical school and who were, presumably, modelling floral pattern dresses all across the country. Somehow, this one had stayed with him for a full five years post-graduation and ended up here, on a wine soaked sofa in Scotland.

"What does it matter who Bill was?" she asked. "The dumb bastard's been dead for what? Four hundred years?"

Four hundred years was the correct answer.

In any case – Sarah insisted – the art of play writing was alive and well and vibrant in this very city. Crispin said something self-deprecating about being one amongst many and Sarah fell back on The Echo.

"How many of the duffers in this place got a column like this?"

"I mean, she's got a point there, Crips," said Duncan, reverting to a name they hadn't used since dissection. "For a salaried GP with Jack at the helm, it's not a complete disaster."

Harry – who did this sort of thing for a living – tried hard to cheer him up.

"Lucy's got the hots for Captain Hook."

Of all the things Harry could have come out with, this was the one that Crispin had least expected.

"That's J M Barrie for you," said Harry, with real confidence. "All kiddie on the outside, deep-seated Freudian nutcase on the inside. He spent most of his 20s running around Kensington Gardens with a toy sword in his hand. Pan's bit of crumpet gets this crush on Captain Hook. Even when she begs him to let her go, she's actually begging for sex. 'Older men, you see. Older men and these wee young lassies. Sometimes they really get it on."

Denying him the pleasure of a smirk, Crispin retained his composure.

"Who I am supposed to be in this one? The Boy who could Fly?"

"Pretty much so, yes," said Harry. "But for Lucy, things are a bit different. Hook represents the excitement and the danger of the adult world. Even if he is missing the odd hand, he's got this boatload of pirates behind him. And for your average Edwardian teenybopper, that counts!"

Crispin reminded Harry that psychoanalysis has no basis in science, that Freud had been put to death by his own GP, and that in the end, Pan does in fact stab Hook just lateral to the xiphi-sternum and throws the little bastard overboard.

"And then the crocodile gets him!" he added, as if for good measure.

"A good thing too!" jeered Duncan. "He bloody well deserves it!"

But Harry was gaining traction.

"What about this Lucy character? Is she going straight down to London for that Globe show?"

Which Lucy was this? The one in real life? Harry nodded and Crispin agreed that she was.

Alert in the kitchen, Duncan made a fresh contribution. "Still no news from Liverpool, I'm afraid. They reckon the books are on their way to Latvia or something."

"Why Latvia?"

Duncan confessed to having made this bit up. The stolen books might be in any country, but they weren't in this one.

Somebody handed out coffee and their conversation progressed to the matter of ransom. Surely the thieves, would try and flog a few volumes back to London as soon as they made it to a non-extradition country.

Crispin hadn't thought of this, but he didn't like the idea and, if he'd had a good view of the street beneath them, his morale might have fallen even further. Diesel engines were cutting in and a long white lorry was preparing to drive down South. The entire RSC production was relocating to *The Globe* and, as soon as they got there, the material contents of the lorry would be transferred to a large store room beneath the stage.

Upbeat between a couple of strong armed drivers, Lucy was looking forward to her trip. The man on her left wore a large and unwieldy dressing above his eye and the one on her right was planning to grin all the way to London.

Six flights up, Crispin sensed that it was time to go, and in the first instance he said goodbye to Duncan. The two men had been friends since medical school, but in the last few weeks, something had changed. Maybe it was the unexpected streak of grey that tainted Duncan's sideburns. Maybe it was the strange exuberance of youth, barn door in so many of their rivals and visibly waning in their own troupe. Whatever, Crispin was left with the feeling that this year's visit to The Fringe might well be their last.

He left through a narrow hallway and so on to an endless, winding staircase. Lingering by the only exit, Sarah called after him, with one last reference to Pan.

"Peter really thinks he can fly back to see Lucy! Every summer."

What a nut.

Pan was a hero to his friends, but he was a fool if he thought Lucy was going to have him in the spring. There aren't any hard men in Nether Nether Land. Only Lost Boys.

Chapter 16

In the event, Crispin reached home before dark. Forsaking such every day luxuries as a coffee, he made excellent time and bludgeoned his lumbar spine in the process. Somewhere outside Derby, he stopped for petrol and stood there, very patiently, whilst the woman behind the desk printed his bill and tried to sign him up for her yoga class. If Crispin wanted the flexibility he really needed, he ought to do yoga.

"Is it really worth it?" she asked, nodding towards his car.

"Oh yes!" he told her, holding out his charge card. "Honestly, it's worth it."

She was only thinking of his health and the doctor thanked her and staggered back towards the Morgan. A few hours later, he was unpacking his bags in Stratford and when he was done, he received a new and unexpected guest.

Jack didn't really need any seeing to. Already familiar with the biscuit tin, he discovered the kettle in a matter of seconds. Once in position, he went on to repeat the same lecture that Crispin had received at the petrol station, pointing out that it was either that or trade in the car. In any case, yoga classes were likely to be dominated by the fairer sex, and surrounding himself with the fairer sex was the way to a better life.

"Well the Morgan didn't work!" sneered Jack, reacting to a filthy look. Neither, Crispin reminded himself, had fifteen minutes of fame, on a rope in Stratford. Maybe it was time for Botox and sit-ups. Jack suggested that they return – this very evening - to the ancient family residence, expanding the offer further with the suggestion of a glass of whisky and a spot of kip in his childhood bed. But Crispin was due on call from midnight and was reluctant to leave the comfort of his own home.

Jack said farewell and Crispin lay down in his largely unnecessary, Grade III listed cottage, desperate for some sort of release. An abundance of REM sleep took him through to the small hours and then, a little after 4am, he awoke very suddenly, as if from a nightmare. When he was a child, the structure of a dream might stay in his head for many days, but as an adult, dreams had passed him by.

This one was different.

Crispin was walking along a path by the river, accompanied by a young woman. Some distance into their journey, he noticed a glass bottle that had been washed up on the riverbank. Leaving the path, he strode through the rushes and retrieved the bottle intact. Then he looked behind him and saw that the girl had stayed on the path, and was shouting down at him in a fit of rage.

Crispin examined the bottle in more detail and found a hand written message. Removing the cork, he shook the message free and called for the girl to join him. She showed no interest, waving him away and disappearing along the path. Still with the letter, Crispin saw that it was addressed to him by name and that it began, as it might well in a dream,

"Dear Son..."

Back in the land of the living, a passing ambulance put an end to his fantasies. Buzzing the cottage on full blast, it bolted him upright in bed.

Christ!

Alone on the edge of the mattress, Crispin cradled his face in the palms of both hands.

Why had the bastards done that now? Could they read his thoughts? Had they waited for this – his moment of maximum vulnerability - then turned on the bell? Hadn't he done enough for all the sick and dying people in this world to be spared by a bunch of paramedics now? Crispin craved the privacy of sleep and a return to his dreams, but knew that he couldn't get there.

It hardly mattered. Shakespeare senior was dead and buried, never to be resurrected and never to engage in conversation again. You couldn't even find him on Facebook. But Crispin had his differences with The Linguists, and he was certain of this: Chekov was wrong. When a man sits down to write, he will *always* project his own opinions onto the page. He can't do anything else. Even when he thinks he's making stuff up, he will still be speaking from the heart. That much was certain. Crispin didn't have much in the way of formal testimony, but he did have his father's novels and the novels were enough.

The doctor rolled over and thought some more.

Who was the girl on the riverbank? Quite possibly, she had been his mother. Although it was likely that his mother was alive, Crispin hadn't heard from her in many years and he couldn't exclude the possibility that she had died some time ago and that no one had told him. On more than one occasion, he had thought about confronting Jack about it, most probably late at night with the old bat was half asleep besides the fire, begging for a new answer.

Thus far, he had never had the balls.

He remembered an oft cited exchange between Ernest Hemingway and his friend, Tennessee Williams. Tennessee asked Ernest how his wife had died and Ernest stayed blank, saying,

"She died, like everybody else does. After that she was dead."

But Crispin didn't even know if his mother was dead, only that she wasn't here and that she would someday die, even if she wasn't there yet. As we all will.

He turned to his bedside clock and tried to calculate how many more hours he would have to wait for the sunrise. It was not yet 4am.

Quite some distance to go.

Chapter 17

The night ended and Crispin held a brief conversation with a colleague on the phone. The colleague in question was about to take over the call and he soon flipped into a rant about a woman who liked to pester them all with mindless trivia. Did Crispin know that patient? Crispin did, although he hadn't heard from her in the night and the guy on the other end felt better for this, steering the conversation to an early end.

It was 8am. He was free of it.

Crispin progressed to the shower, and then a heavily creased towel and then he dressed – very slowly – for the day that awaited him. A brief drive through the countryside soon followed and a short while later, he parked outside the broad, Victorian home that had once defined his youth.

It wasn't that bad. On the day they gave him the deeds, Jack's house had come with a row of defunct stables. Somewhere in between the nurturing of his own offspring and his one, slightly hapless nephew, Jack had found time to refurbish the stables and make horses an integral part of their lives. In recent years, Jack's energy had sometimes faltered and in a chair by an open fire he could get through a quarter of a bottle of whisky on his own. Besides the horses and the hesitant words of his wife, single malt whisky was the only prop he had ever asked for, and Crispin would have been loath to take it from him.

The nephew knocked on the door and in a matter of seconds, the accidental figure of Jack had taken him in. Strolling through the house and on to the paddock, Crispin discovered his favourite mare and moved – like a reflex - to touch her face.

"*Daisy,*" said Jack, as if – by some freak coincidence – he might have forgotten. Daisy was beautiful and had long cast a spell over any man who met her. "I raised her from a foal." Again, this was common knowledge, but Jack was onto a different line. "The newsmen were looking for you?" Conscious that this might have been his own doing, Crispin became sheepish. "Abrasive little bastards," said the Uncle. "The lot of them! They gave your aunt quite a fright!"

Crispin said something about time and the short attention span of the press, and Jack shied away from real friction, saying only, "These things happen."

These things happen.

Some years ago now, Jack had been stabbed in the stomach by one of his own patients. Flat on the floor with a knife wound, Jack had elected to play dead rather than fight back. That's the party line these days. Fighting back just doesn't appear in your average job description and the family doctors of this world are expected to fake death whenever they find a patient with a grudge. Ignoring the NHS protocol, Crispin had learnt some kind of deadly hand thrust to the neck in the TA, and had often fantasied about having a go in his *well man clinic*. Thus far, no one had turned up with a bread knife and chance had never come his way.

Daisy sneezed very loudly and Crispin moved closer to calm her down. It worked, and a long and ashen face rushed through his hands.

"You know," said Jack, "a while ago now, they had that big fuss about the Hitler Diaries. In the end, it turned out some looney had faked the whole thing! I think he did it for the money." Sensing a fall in Crispin's spirits, Jack did his best to shore them up. "Did you fake climbing down that hole?" Crispin had not. "A lot of people wouldn't have done. 'Gone down a hole, I mean. If you'd driven on by, nobody would have thought less of you. Life's like that. Nobody ever got it in the neck for being ordinary. When you do something different, when you try to stand out from the crowd, that's when they come after you."

"What if they do?" asked Crispin. "Nobody cares. The things in that hole nearly killed this town. The tourist board were having kittens."

"What about the TA?" asked Jack, who understood his nephew much better than his nephew would ever know. "Can't you do something with them?"

"There's only so much fun you can have in a dug-out."

A little further along, Jack spied his daughter, tall and attentive besides a second, truly beautiful horse.

"Unlike *Popeye* here," said Jack, stroking the next pony's face. "Who is endless fun for anyone who ever rode her."

Crispin's cousin turned and smiled. Barely 19, she lived for horses. "Hello, Crispin!"

It was a cold welcome, but it was verbal contact and Crispin responded in kind. "'Karen. 'Working hard?"

She was not. Being alive in the presence of a horse could never be described as work. Not for Karen. Most of her life, she seemed not to notice Crispin and had probably spoken purely out of deference to her father's presence. He remembered her as a stand-in for his much younger sibling, angry in a distant corner. Today, she was almost a woman, but Crispin wouldn't claim to know her, then or now.

But Jack Shakespeare didn't keep horses as an act of altruism. He was paying good money for these animals and they were going to have to work for it. The men saddled up and mounted their respective steeds, blissfully unaware of the threat that awaited them.

Crispin's action in Scotland had not gone unnoticed and as far as Arthur Kranz was concerned, both members of the Shakespeare family were legitimate targets. From the second they first left the paddock, Crispin and Jack were being watched through telescopic sights of a deadly weapon.

Jack's adherence to ritual was well known in these parts and today would be no different. First a narrow road that led to the field, then a gentle slope and the sudden spurt that took them down to the river. Even if Crispin had declined to join him, the general feeling in the Kranz camp was that Jack would have saddled up anyway, and that if either man was hit, then Crispin would remain in Stratford until long after Kranz had finished his work in England.

The horses gained speed and the range narrowed. There might have been a slight headwind and Al – who had fired a crossbow before – waited for it to fade.

Slowing down, Jack returned to the matter in hand: his nephew. The only boy in his far from ordinary clan. "I'd always hoped you'd spend more time in Stratford."

"What was he like?" asked Crispin, before Jack could continue. "My father."

"Same as all these creative types, I suppose. Only more so. 'Tormented souls, artists. If they aren't tormented, they don't have anything to write about. 'Took it too far though. My brother was more interested in writing than he was in living. Unlike his son, who seems more interested in living than doing any sort of work at all."

"And what did they think?" asked Crispin. "When he packed in medicine?"

The extended family, it emerged, believed he was bonkers. But Jack wasn't so sure. "Some of his stuff is still in print. *You're* still reading it. If he hadn't gone to an early grave, he might just have broken through."

Jack asked about the decidedly ex-lodger in Crispin's cottage and how he had managed to lose track of her so quickly.

"She's gone to London."

It was a poignant question and Crispin bowed his head in thought, saving his life in the process. The bolt from a distant cross bow brushed softly against his cheek and struck his Uncle in the shoulder.

"*Jack!*"

He'd been hit. In another month, he might have been more heavily dressed and by implication, the bolt might have failed to penetrate his jacket. But this was August and the missile had lodged very easily, just above the collar bone. Wailing on the receiving end of it all, Jack lost his balance and went down to the grass.

It was time for action. Glancing up from his Uncle, Crispin saw a lone figure on the edge of the meadow. The figure stood upright, carrying what Crispin took to be a crossbow. Moments later, he disappeared into the tree line. Having previously merely trotted across this field, Crispin switched to full gallop now.

Approaching the edge of the tree line, he saw a 4-wheel drive and watched it pull away. The dirt tracks that skirted the meadow were rarely used and it was unlikely that there would be anything there to hit him. He decided to take the first row of bushes on Daisy, coming down blind on the boggy slopes beyond and maintaining pursuit on the flat.

The jeep gained ground and Crispin conceded the obvious. One man on a horse can't catch a motorised vehicle on the flat. Doubtless Winston had already reached the same conclusion and was preparing to go up a gear when a battered Volkswagen Camper Van came out from nowhere and threatened to spoil his day. The camper van braked, violently and a collision was narrowly avoided as the drivers skidded along their respective dykes.

The gap narrowed and Crispin had some kind of strong arm fantasy about forcing his way into the jeep and punching his opponent in the face. But his chance was only fleeting and the jeep was soon back on the flat and veering right.

In any case, the chase was almost over. A low hanging beam rushed across the roof of the jeep and swung briskly towards the man on horseback. At the last minute, Crispin loosened his feet in the stirrups and steeled himself for the worse. Daisy made it through, but he didn't, swaying forward as the branch took him. Chasing the jeep was, perhaps, the dumbest thing he'd done since his second rag week and he was lucky to survive intact.

The branch wasn't particularly helpful either, cracking loudly and discarding Crispin on the dirt track where he waited for Daisy to double back and find him. In time, she did and the two of them turned around and scrambled up the escarpment, onto the flat and into the thigh high grass that coated the meadow.

Chapter 18

Stratford has long been graced by its own Infirmary, although decades of rationalisation have reduced the place to the status of a cottage hospital. More serious trauma is diverted to Warwick and the men who came to help Jack in the meadow saw him as major trauma indeed. Fully familiar with the routine, Crispin had dialled the relevant numbers and made no attempt to move the patient himself.

In other circumstances, Crispin might have boarded the ambulance and asked to drive to Warwick with them, but there was nothing he could do to help and in any case, there was still the matter of the horses. Having stabled the two of them, Crispin took time to update his cousins and to try and reassure them that their father wasn't actually dead. At least not yet.

Remember that time when he played dead for some halfwit with a knife? Well, this was much the same. Just a different kind of knife.

It wasn't his best ever gag and when Karen tried to do laughter, he had to stand there and watch her do tears.

And so Crispin moved on, first to a drizzly car park in Warwick, and then to a quiet side room in the district general hospital. There, he rested in a government issue armchair and spoke very calmly to a rather earnest looking police officer with a notepad and pen, and a complete inability to smile. Unexpectedly, the officer refused to accept his account of the shooting. In particular, he seemed completely hung up on the issue of motive. What motive might anyone have to shoot an unknown GP in Stratford?

The prospects of a disgruntled patient soon emerged and Crispin didn't like the idea. Hadn't Jack been attacked by someone else on his own list? Warwickshire police had already pulled his file and found evidence of a previous stabbing. Maybe this was all part of a pattern.

"Would you say he was the sort of man who had a poor rapport with his patients?"

Things might have gotten worse had it not been for the arrival of a middle-aged woman in blue, fully equipped with the kind of NHS tea trolley that no one in the private sector would have even considered serving tea from. Receiving his beverage with a forceful smile, Crispin began to sip, very politely, whilst the police officer inflamed the situation further by bringing up money.

"If this fellow should die, am I correct in assuming that you yourself are due to inherit his entire practice?"

Crispin threw him a dirty look and the officer tried another approach. Crispin had been in the news a lot recently. Why was that?

Passive in his NHS chair, Crispin hoped for Jack's survival, if only to serve as a corroborative witness. Meanwhile, the police officer just didn't want to stop.

"Are you able to identify either of the men in the bushes?"

Crispin could not.

"But you're sure there were two?"

Crispin wasn't sure, but the officer was, describing a double line of footprints in the mud and Crispin became strangely silent, acknowledging, perhaps for the first time, that the man with the crossbow really did have had an accomplice. If this were the case, then one of them might have fired from the car whilst the other took the wheel.

"They were wearing hoods," he added, trying hard to stick with the plural.

"Hoodies?"

"No. Balaclava helmets."

A second police officer arrived. This was Higgins, the same man who had delivered the first press conference after the heist in Stratford, and he made a show of taking offence when Crispin pretended not to recognise him.

"Crossbow bolt to the chest!" said Inspector Higgins, almost – but not quite – scornful. "Not an especially common occurrence in these parts. Can you think of any reason why any person – or persons - might want to kill your Uncle?"

Crispin could not, responding as he did with an emphatic, "*No!*"

It wasn't enough.

"Aren't you the same man who discovered these books in the first place?" asked the Inspector.

But for Crispin, this was too much.

"Aren't you the same man who can't find them now?" In fact, Higgins was exactly that man although he managed to avoid saying so out loud. "Are you any better at finding a nutter with a grudge?"

"Actually," chuckled Higgins, "I think you'll find my men are already dealing with these *documents,* you mention."

Losing patience with the police, Crispin abandoned the chair and strode towards the door. If they weren't planning to charge him, they couldn't detain him. He felt a sense of duty to his extended family and it was time to play it out.

Chapter 19

In the popular imagination, the National Health Service is a child of the Second World War and in its formative years, the organisation leant heavily on the ethos of that conflict. Even today, shared bays are pretty much the norm and the older generation is noticeably more at ease than the young.

But when the patient is a member of staff, the nurses will usually offer them a side room and this was the case for Uncle Jack, who Crispin had now encountered, surrounded by his relatives. Over to one side, Jack's sad, National Health Service porridge was largely untouched and on balance, Crispin saw this as a good thing. Resting in the corner, he glanced at the old man's torso and checked for signs of life.

It was still moving.

None of the aunts spoke and after about ten minutes, Crispin started looking for some other form of distraction. Two feet above them, the last cathode ray tube in England was blaring on mute, with subtitles for the hard of hearing.

"The search for the missing Stratford documents continues. Scotland Yard are trying to contact the American Art Historian, Arthur Kranz."

Right on cue, a full colour picture of 'Arthur Kranz' flashed up on the screen. To a man with a vested interest in the material, this was gripping stuff, but not quite gripping enough to tear him away from his duty.

That duty included sitting in a circle besides a man who didn't even know they were there. It's not a great way to spend your afternoon and Crispin soon developed an intimate fascination with the polystyrene tiles on the roof. How many were there? How had they been stuck on and why hadn't anybody bothered to dust them down in the last twenty five years? More to the point, why had Crispin abandoned his uncle in a field in pursuit of a vehicle that he couldn't hope to catch? To get himself shot? To delay calling the ambulance by another ten minutes?

Cowering in a badly torn NHS chair, Crispin tried to convince himself that he would never be so reckless again, at least, not in a scenario where he was likely to be caught. Indeed, Crispin might well have come in for a real slating on this one, but as fate might have it, his extended family were psyching themselves up for a different fight. His Great Aunt Jemma, had taken a dislike to one of the nurses and was determined to stay in the building until she had found some way to hit out at her. Petrifying at the opposite end of the circle, Great Aunt Sal was of much the same opinion and had several very practical ideas as to how this could be done. None of them sounded like a lot of fun to Crispin and he started praying that the nurse's shift might end before any of his relatives could get to her.

Then, without warning, he received a sensitive phone call from Sarah. Sarah talked about Jack, about the risks inherent to any inpatient stay and an idealised treatment for the DTs. Crispin blushed very faintly at the DT bit and tried to remember if he had ever mentioned this one before. Either that or she'd picked it up on physical signs. Either way, he promised to raise it with the staff.

The thing that had always shocked him about delirium tremens was the spiders. All around the world there are people drying out, and quite a lot of them start to hallucinate about spiders. Never a bird or a rat or a T-Rex, always a bunch of spiders. Nobody knows why. Some of them start to scream and brush them away, but the only real treatment is another shot of whisky. Now that Sarah had brought it up, Crispin was suddenly worried about the number of witnesses in this room. No matter how bad things get with the bottle, it doesn't really matter so long as no one finds out, but this place was positively crawling with second degree relatives. He felt an unexpected impulse to run down to the off license and come back with something hard. No one really wants an NHS cup of tea and Jack would appreciate that.

And then he hung up, much too quickly and immediately regretted his actions. This was the problem with being a medic.

His friends would always understand.

Crispin chose to keep cool with the help of his smart phone and he soon progressed to his photo album, where the winning smile of his lodger came back to greet him.

It was a well framed, if slightly blurred image and he decided to give himself full marks for spacial awareness. Lucy stood alone by the Morgan with a single streetlight well above her head. She was in Stratford and there was some sort of grey smudge just behind her left ear. You get this with camera phone pictures in the dark, but if you aren't sure what it is, you can always blow it up. Expanding the image with two fingers, Crispin saw the shadowy figure of Arthur and his wooden box at the rear of a long white lorry.

The doctor froze, the chatter of aunts suddenly vanquished from his mind. This was a real game changer and it was time for a new and original approach. Standing upright again, he leant forward to check his uncle's pulse. It was there, alright. The charts on the end of the bed were reassuring too and a few seconds later, he shouted back over his shoulder as he dashed for the exit.

"He'll be alright in a minute!"

Lacking the energy to move, his aged relatives remained seated whilst a state owned door swung loudly on its hinges. In the end, it fell to Great Aunt Jemma to offer this verdict on an unplanned departure.

"That's the *Shakespeares* for you!"

That was indeed the Shakespeares for you and the youngest one amongst them was already in the car park and calling his friend. An electronic answering service suggested that Tom's number had been deactivated, but this wasn't likely. Doubtless Tom was shagging one of his rowing team. The historic city of Cambridge was less than two hours away and Crispin needed to get there in daylight.

Chapter 20

Having reconvened in the British capital, Kranz's men had been compelled to find a third and final base for their enterprise. Concerned about face recognition, Kranz had delegated the search to Gary, who had yet to pop up on the police radar and who had done much to reassure their all but innocent landlord. A large and essentially empty warehouse had been signed over for the best part of a month, although Kranz himself was planning to be out of here in a matter of days. Well to the east of central London, this latest base was a dirty, dingy little hang out, just weeks away from full scale gentrification. The top floor offered a wonderful view of the Thames, albeit in its broad, industrial back water.

Their next phase would also require more man power and Winston had recruited some solid individuals from South London. Well paid but largely ignorant as to their objective, the newcomers loitered in the warehouse and waited for orders.

Alone with his lap top, Kranz had already logged-on to the local press in Stratford. A tiny caption bloated out on his screen and Kranz took time to study the attached image. As is the norm for a tabloid headline, the language was direct:

DOCTOR STRUCK BY CROSSBOW BOLT

The legislation on crossbows was surprisingly vague and it was a matter of some concern to the press that an enemy of the medical profession had been able to arm himself with such a weapon. The local MP was sitting on a distinctly marginal seat and had already pledged to raise it in The House. Whatever the response, it would be too late for Uncle Jack, who was unlikely to leave hospital before the autumn.

Kranz swept one hand across his chin. Having omitted to shave since his raid on the dig, he had acquired a reasonable beard. Kranz hadn't spoken to the British Museum staff since the day he left Stratford and the police were bound to be looking for him. The beard would serve him well.

Then, suddenly, there was action. Winston and Al announced their approach with the help of a creaking staircase and a desperate wheeze. Al wasn't in the mood to knock and when the door burst open, their initial reception was cold. Hesitant in the hallway, an American asthmatic reached in his pocket and drew deeply on his inhaler. Winston stood silent besides him and the rest of the gang waited patiently whilst their badly flawed tough guy, coughed a bit more. Neither man had covered themselves in glory in Scotland and if they'd been half as hard as Kranz had taken them for, the diaries would already be his.

Slumping heavily on a wooden chair, Al produced the crossbow from his bag and let it clang heavily against the table. Further to the right, and much colder to touch, lay a large black handgun.

Arthur sighed into his laptop, seeing the chance to comment.

"How did a Harvard Professor phrase it? Put a baseball cap on a man's head and you drop his IQ by ten points. Turn it around and it drops by another twenty."

The new arrivals looked up in unison and the rest of the gang burst into laughter.

"You can laugh now! You can laugh now!" snapped Winston, "but how'd we get into this mess in the first place? If we'd waited 'till they had 'em in that Museum, if we'd waited 'till they'd brought these bleedin' books down to London, it 'ave been a straight forward thing. A heist movie! I've got friends who've done banks. I've got friends who've broken into them rich Russian types in Fulham. My boys would have got into that Museum in next to no time!"

If this was rebellion then Kranz took it well.

"I know that museum." He told them. "I know that museum, and I know how they work! And I'm telling you now, you'd never have come out with more than one volume. The damned things would have been scattered on every level. This is the best way. Everything that matters is in that one box and this is a soft target. The books are in our sights boys, and it's time to get them back!"

The room fell silent again and Al, who had long harboured doubts about the Kranz plan, nodded in blind agreement.

Chapter 21

Meanwhile, about an hour north of London, Crispin had left the A14 and was sliding from one nameless roundabout to the next. There are a lot of gifted people in Cambridge, but not many of them work in Town Planning and in its outskirts, the city has little to say for itself. As a seat of learning, Cambridge is close to the very top of the international league table and in an historical sense, it easily predates The Bard. There is, however, no reason to suppose that Shakespeare studied at this or any other university. His was the University Of Life, and in the course of time, he would matriculate with a double First.

Having arrived in the early evening, Crispin pulled up in a suitably authentic alleyway and started to raise the hood. The tourist crowd was fading out and a stream of real life students were drifting back to their dorms. Besides his parking space there was a large pole and on top of the pole, there was a tiny white sign demanding 20 pence for every minute he decided to park here. Alternatively, he could wait another six minutes and escape all fees. Tempted though he was, Crispin decided to stand by his vehicle and avoid the fine. Crispin worked hard for his money and didn't see why he should hand it over to Cambridge City Council.

That isn't to say his time by the parking meter was wasted. Six minutes was, for example, more than enough time to plan his approach to Tom. In any case, the worse parking fine on offer was unlikely to exceed 50 quid and it was hard to imagine that the Diaries would go for anything less than £50 million. And if there was a message in his waiting, it was a sad one. *Deep down* – Crispin knew that his diaries were already lost.

He looked up. It was 6:30. 'Time to get going.

A minute or so later, the doctor came to a halt besides a generous wooden door. Someone had wedged the thing half open, and it seemed to Crispin that the door was a portal to another world. The garden inside had caught the sun in much the same way that most of the rest of the gardens in England couldn't and everything on offer was perfect. He saw a carefully tended lawn and row of flowers with yellow stamens and bright red petals. Just above that, he saw a row of marble steps that led up to the college chapel. Like the fleeting smile of a pretty girl, the garden held his attention for much longer than it really should have done and Crispin felt the urge to reboot his life and sign on for a place at Cambridge from the age of 18.

He couldn't. Eighteen has been and gone and we can never have it back. Leaving the door behind him, he walked a little further and found the far end of the building where another perfect lawn came right up to the edge of the wall. When Crispin looked up, he saw that most of the stones were buried in a rich coat of ivy. Above that, there was a small balcony, and as far as Crispin was concerned, this represented a point of entry to Tom's lab. Getting there would be a tad harder than his descent into the sinkhole and in the first instance, he decided to try the main entrance.

Sadly, the University had other ideas.

"Can I help you?"

Its first line of defence was a scrawny little man with a polished scalp, boring in a fancy wooden pillbox. By the looks of things, the pillbox dated back to the 1950's and Crispin rather liked it. The backs of the man's hands were stained with the fading joy of a dead tattoo and something in his manner suggested that help was the last thing on this planet he would ever deliver.

"Yes," said Crispin. "I'd like to speak to Tom. That's Doctor Tom Edwards? I think he works here."

"He's busy!"

"In what sense?"

The man in the pill box said something about diligence, high achievement and the global significance of Tom's work. And then his eyes darted back to the voluptuous wee lassy on Page Three, and he said, "Now, sod off!"

"So, who's busy, right now?"

"Doctor Edwards!" said the man. "I'm under orders to keep the lot of you away from him. He's expecting to get on top of something very important."

"Right."

But the man in the pill box was just that little bit naive. Less than fifty feet away, Tom had amassed the resources to tackle almost any challenge in his field and at this very moment, he was tackling recreational sex. Having explored this area throughout his Doctorate, Tom knew that the floor of a sealed research lab was as good a place as any for a quick shag and far more cost effective than the local bed and breakfast. Inches from his left ear, his laptop was linked to a loud speaker and playing a golden oldie.

"I'm dying for love, I need a physician
bring him on board and he'll see my condition."

Meanwhile, out on the wall, Crispin heard the lyrics first and the heavy breathing second. This particular challenge was proving a bit harder than he had expected and he was close to climbing back down and ram raiding the pillbox. Clinging to the gaps between the stone, Crispin struggled to name the band.

"Christ, he *is* shagging one of his rowing team!"

In any case, he had other things on his mind. The historic masonry offered far fewer footholds than he had hoped for and Crispin felt the need to change tactics and grab the foliage.

It worked. Better than that, it reminded him of a scene from one of the early Jason Bourne movies although, again, he couldn't actually remember which one. In the circumstances, it might have been better to maintain a holding pattern whilst the music played out, but then, suddenly, the ivy began to tear free. It was time for decisive action. Scrambling up and over the balcony,

Crispin rolled through the window and onto the cold floorboards.

"Tom!" he heard a woman giggle, with a surprise foreign accent. "I could do with a doctor right now."

Looking to one side, Tom recognised his new arrival and took it very well.

"It's funny you should say that!"

Chapter 22

Crispin brushed himself down and Tom expressed a passing interest in his technique.

"Did you use the ivy?"

Crispin had. The bald bloke in the pill box had proven difficult and Tom apologised on his behalf. There have – Tom informed him - always been barriers to access in Cambridge, but it was good to know that a determined figure like Crispin could still overcome them.

Concerned about time, Crispin raised the issue of Carbon 14, but Tom wasn't ready for that. Instead, he wanted to tell him about the backstory on the bald man in the pill box, starting with his subscriptions to a string of specialist web pages.

"Things have been getting gradually worse since he bought that tablet. When he only had the laptop, he was a bit more cautious. Now he's got that tablet, he thinks he can get away with anything."

"Well, yes," said Crispin, trying not to roll his eyes.

Over to one side, the girl with the foreign accent had gone to fill the kettle and find some underwear. Glancing in her general direction, Tom made some sort of minor adjustments to his belt buckle.

"You know," he hissed, "the original patent for the tea bag was actually filed in Germany." Crispin must have looked blank because Tom nodded towards the kitchen again, adding, "Christine's from Cologne."

This was all very interesting, but not as interesting as the picture that Crispin had just seen on Tom's wall. It was the same monochrome image that hung in Crispin's living room and time had done nothing to erase its tone. But Tom wasn't interested in the photograph. He was talking about the missing diaries and leading Crispin to a nearby bench and a very impressive bit of kit. This was presumably, the mythical Carbon-14 machine that had – for so long –

dominated his work. Waiting on the boot up, Tom took a look at Crispin's smart phone and the night time shot of Lucy in Stratford. The lorry, Arthur Kranz, and the Morgan were all up there on the screen.

"God almighty!"

"Can you believe it?"

"And she's actually paying you to live in that cottage?"

"*No!*" groaned Crispin, who had long struggled with Tom's libido. "Not her! The guy behind her!"

Tom turned to the kitchen again. His professorial kettle was making steam and the sight of it seemed to calm his nerves.

"There's a car and a lorry." said Tom, back with the picture. "And it's dark."

"And there's a man with a lorry and a box."

"That's what people do with lorries, Crispin. They load them up with boxes. If people didn't have boxes to load up, they wouldn't bother making all these lorries."

"Arthur isn't into haulage."

"And if that is this American guy – Arthur as you keep calling him – why would he have done that? Why load this package into that lorry, when he's only just nicked it?"

"Because that was his plan. They'd already closed off the area."

"Except for the HGVs! They were too small to worry about?"

"Precisely!"

"You know, they tracked down the van? All burnt out to kill the DNA. Why'd he do a thing like that?"

"As a decoy," snapped Crispin. "And it worked. The police are still down by the docks, strip searching the Scousers."

"And the evidence?" asked Tom. "Do you have any hard evidence for all of this?"

As a matter of fact, *Hard Evidence* was exactly what had brought Crispin to this lab and he quickly produced the only bit on offer. It was the folded sheet of paper he had salvaged from the cellar, four weeks and a thousand years ago.

Mulling the thing over with a hand held lens, Tom started to think out loud.

"So, in theory, this could be it?" he said. "The Great Man's hand, I mean?" Crispin agreed and Tom decided to ramble. "You know, for ages, people used to look at that Turin Shroud thing and pretend it was *His* face. Then they ran a couple of strands through the Carbon-14 machine and it turned out to be 900 years old. A narrow miss by about ten centuries." He tossed the fragment in his fingers, as if it might be possible to date the thing from this action alone. "It's not that big. You know, we're going to have to scrub the whole page if you want to date it?" Crispin did and Tom stuffed the whole page into the Carbon-14 machine and tightened the door with a tiny crow bar. A few minutes later, lights flickered, and the room was possessed by a gentle tremor. Over by the window, they could see gas spouting through an external duct. Hard data – Crispin sensed – was fast approaching.

Fast but not yet. In the meantime, Crispin's attention returned to the kitchen. Like Tom, Christine had tried to style herself as some sort of later day undergraduate. Theirs was a beautifully crafted image that reminded Crispin of the sales brochure for an Ivy League design studio. *Tom Ford*, maybe *Gant*. 'Hard to say which. Whatever, his host had followed his line of sight and the staring thing had to end.

"Were you surprised she was German?"

Crispin did his best to stay calm. "Sort of." he mumbled. "A bit."

"I'll bet you couldn't guess that from the bonking noises alone."

Crispin agreed that this would have been difficult and Tom was visibly thrilled.

"I mean," said Crispin, "are you meant to be able to tell? Just from the noise?"

But Tom was back on his feet, darting over to his teutonic partner and faking interest in the tea bags. Crispin watched him stoop to caress her waist and decided to look away. This was bad news. Charging down the A14, he had hoped to recruit Tom as an active accomplice in his adventures. Not now. Not anymore. This guy was never going to leave Cambridge.

Crispin asked Tom what they were looking for.

"Carbon 14," said Tom, as if Crispin didn't know. "Isn't that what you wanted?"

This was the kind of thing Tom liked doing. 'Talking about technical stuff he already understood.

Carbon 14 is manufactured on a daily basis in the Earth's atmosphere. There, light from the Sun collides with the nitrogen atoms, creating an unstable isotope of carbon. Plants and animals absorb carbon for as long as it takes them to die, and from that moment on, the isotope proves unstable and its presence in the dead tissue begins to fade. For the scrap of paper in Tom's machine, the start date had been the time of the felling of an Elizabethan tree. By measuring the residual activity tonight, Tom would be able to count back to that day.

"Did you follow that?"

Crispin had, although to be fair, he already knew it.

"Of course," said Tom, "we can't be sure the writer didn't use old paper. 'Like, he inherited a pile of the stuff from his grandmother, then he didn't get round to using it till he got old."

"Can't we date it from the ink?" asked Crispin, suddenly very worried.

"Not now we've set fire to it, no."

Then, for the first time, Christine began to speak. "But could it last that long?"

"Well, Crispin thinks his books are good for four hundred years!"

Hunched forward on a wooden stool, Crispin recalled the morning that had changed his life.

"It was the nearest thing to me. I just reached out and grabbed it."

"Grabbed what?" asked Tom, pointing to the box in his Carbon-14 machine. "This piece of paper?"

Crispin nodded.

"You know, the police are calling it in at 1780. 'On the radio. That would put it out by two hundred years. Not as dumb as the Turin Shroud, but a bit of a shit for all the Bard fanatics on the planet."

"Tom?" said Crispin, "Do you have some kind of deep seated prejudice against the Tudors?"

"I'm afraid so," said Tom, pausing only to sip on his tea. "If you'd wanted to get me down that hole, it would have to have been BC. In fact, it would have had to have been BC *and* Greek. Otherwise, I'd have stayed in the Morgan.

"Crispin raised his smartphone and did his best to look intense. "It's *him,* Tom! It's the man in this photograph. I saw him last week in Scotland."

Concerned that it might be left out of the conversation, the Carbon-14 Machine decided to bleep, very loudly in E Flat. This was poignant timing. What had once been paper was now only dust, but the data that Crispin so hoped for was up there on the screen.

"There you go," said Tom. "It's not worth dying for. '1600 to 1620. 'Might just be Elizabethan. What are you suggesting it could be? A diary?" Tom took his silence to mean *yes*. "And if you're right," he demanded, much more loudly, "and it is a diary, what are you going to gain from this adventure that you haven't already got?"

Crispin put down his tea cup and prepared to deliver his big speech.

"If you had to name a book," he began, "one book that changed the way we think, not just here, but throughout the English speaking world. What would that book be?"

Sadly for Crispin, Tom knew this one too. "The King James II Bible," he called, dabbing the corners of his mouth with a fancy tea towel. "Final answer."

"A book by *one* man?"

The archaeologist put his hands up: "*The First Folio.*"

The First Folio was the correct answer and the lab fell briefly silent.

"A diary is a unique document," said Tom. "It's not a poem or a novel. It's a data stream from another man's life."

Once again, Christine called out from the sidelines: "Why are you telling him that? Isn't that why he's here?"

"Well, for one thing," said Tom, "it might not be a good read. If you track this thing down and someone puts it on the web, every Shakespeare buff on the planet is going to go nuts! Nuts in the negative sense of the word. Do you know who this guy was?"

Crispin didn't. If he already knew, he wouldn't be looking for his diaries.

"Think about it!" said Tom, as if in warning. "He probably had shares in the slave trade. Pissed himself laughing whenever he saw the Welsh! Do you think he was best mates with Marlowe? They were probably taking it up the butt together on the Tuesday morning and calling for the death penalty for arse bandits by the Wednesday afternoon."

"Why the hell would they do that?"

"Because he was a *human being*! And that's what human beings do. They aren't *saints*. They're bastards! They-are-of-their-time! Even if you're right and this thing is real, you're not looking for a hagiography. It's a *diary.*"

"But then we'll know *the truth*." groaned Crispin.

Suddenly, Tom's exasperation became a physical thing, his fingers tearing through uncombed hair.

"Nobody wants *the truth*!"

"Then why do you keep digging the stuff up?"

"That's different!" said Tom, much more calmly. "I'm a professional. I can handle the truth. Where you're going, there isn't going to be any truth! Just pissed off luvies, shitting on their hero 'cause he said the wrong thing." And then, more quietly, Tom tried a different line. Something that Crispin could not have foreseen. "Assuming you survive."

A cold silence engulfed the lab. Tom looked into Crispin's eyes and played his last card.

"You know it pointless doing all this for the girl? A book, yes. But not a girl! An actress can *never* be a credible partner in life. These people are all messed up! *All* messed up. 'A thespian could make my rowing team look stable! Why do you think they all end up in the divorce courts? Overdosed? Dead in the bath? They're cute, sure! 'Course they're cute! But they're a waste of space." Again, the doctor failed to react and Tom decided to give him his dues. "You've *got* to go to London."

"I'm almost skint," said Crispin.

"Oh, you can make it down to London. I'm sure," said Tom, who had already given him some data and had never given anybody money. "Besides, if it's a bed you're looking for, you can always call Roger."

This was a special and rarely mentioned name. The two men turned to a black and white photograph on the wall. It was indeed an exact copy of the picture in Crispin's house. The same three numskulls, all of them livid by the same paper towel machine. First Crispin, then Tom and then an odd looking character on the far right.

"Do you think he'd want me to come?"

"I should think he'd be in his elephant. Flaunting his furniture, telling you where to stand. Besides, it's not as if he can't afford it.

Whilst Tom and Crispin were still debating, the man who could afford it was relaxed on the top floor of his New Build Apartment Block, just a short distance from a great waterway. Tom's phone call caught him alone in a designer dressing gown and if the bill for this one garment had been diverted into Crispin's current account, it could have covered his mortgage for the best part of a month. A row of neatly pressed sports jackets ordained his half-open wardrobe and along the floor, a gratuitous line of footwear streamed out towards the door.

Tom asked Roger if Crispin could stay for a while and Roger put on a transient show of anger before practically begging him to come down. After a challenging night on Tom's floor, Stratford's most esteemed General Practitioner awoke with the sun and descended to the lawn with the help of a makeshift rope. It was a brief but well executed manoeuvre that won immediate praise from the man on the balcony.

"Awesome," whispered Tom, coiling back the rope in his lab. "It's not even a proper rope."

It wasn't a proper rope, but it was the only thing they could find on the day and Crispin took pride in his ability to improvise. Waving from the grass, he skipped back to the main street and paused briefly, to get a better view of the archetypal beggar, cross legged and neat besides the Morgan. The beggar had a crumpled sleeping bag behind him and a gritty mongrel that was there to ward off loneliness. His paper backed book carried a jet black spine and Crispin had to tear himself away from the title.

Only in Cambridge do the beggars read Dostoevsky.

Climbing into his car, the doctor turned the key.

Chapter 23

About 15 miles short of London, the M11 ascends a gentle hill and at the summit of that hill, the driver is rewarded with an extraordinary view of the capital. Dull towers leap into low hanging cloud, and a little piece of Docklands does its best to ape Manhattan.

Four hundred years ago, Crispin's namesake had said goodbye to Stratford and set out upon this same journey. How long had it taken? Where and when had he stopped for food and lodgings? Nobody knew. Doubtless, he had done it all on foot, but for some reason Crispin liked to see the guy on a horse. The London that awaited him would have been smaller than modern Plymouth and the bulk of its inhabitants could barely read and write. And yet, from within that same gene pool, the Elizabethans would produce an army of poets, the likes of which the world had never seen before.

What were the forces that acted in Shakespeare's life to drive him on this quest? Surely, it would have been easier to stay in Stratford and make a go of his father's glove business? Did his parents despise him for leaving? Had they sponsored his trip? Nobody really knew, although from where Crispin was sitting, the decision seemed entirely rational.

The motorway ended and Crispin was quickly engulfed by the urban sprawl. He followed the road signs as far as the river and then turned abruptly right. Weaving his way between the warehouses of a bygone age, he passed the iconic Flood Barrier that shielded the city from the waves. It was a particularly striking bit of kit and on a better day, he might have felt inclined to pull up and check the place out in detail, but Crispin was short on time and he had just spotted a crucial road sign: 'DOCKLANDS'.

A few minutes later, he was parked outside a new and imposing block of flats on the North bank of the Thames.

Here, his former flat mate, Roger, had built a life and a world of his own, separate from the medical and separate from the academic world of Cambridge. The door to the foyer opened without prompting and Crispin was quickly greeted by a man with an open can of beer. Roger had followed Crispin's approach to the foyer using a CCTV camera and synchronised the cracking of the can with the exact instant that Crispin reached the entrance. It was a difficult thing to do, but Roger had done it anyway and was waiting for some sort of praise from his guest.

Sadly, Crispin was too gobsmacked to notice the beer.

"*God Almighty!* Is this yours?"

In Crispin's mind, Roger's very name was synonymous with that desperate little tenement they had once shared in South London, adorned as it was with rising damp and pink graffiti. The contrast between then and now just couldn't have been greater, but Roger hadn't done with his beer. 'Specifically, the can, the cost of buying the thing in bulk and the origins of its distinctive graphic. In short this was no ordinary can of beer.

"I know it tastes ordinary." said Roger. "But it isn't."

"I can see," said Crispin, drinking wildly and checking out the kitchen. Roger had a pair of Filipino cleaners in on a regular basis. The place was spotless.

"Did you know this building won an award?"

"Christ, really? Was it a famous one?"

"No," said Roger, quite firmly. "It wasn't a very famous one. But it was an award."

They drifted to the balcony and Roger gave names to each of the important landmarks in turn, until he was all out of landmarks and there was nothing left to do except talk about his Aston Martin.

How many Aston Martins did Crispin suppose they made in a week?

Crispin wasn't sure. Unexpectedly, Roger seemed to baulk at this one too, but he soon came up with an approximate figure of nine. Possibly ten. Anyway, it wasn't very many and within a matter of seconds, Roger had thought of something else. It was, he announced, time to discard their special beer cans and dash off for Lucy's stage play.

"What, right now?"

"Isn't that why you came here?"

"Yes."

"Well, let's go."

Crispin trailed Roger down to the Marina and Roger introduced him to his very own, hand-built Italian speedboat.

"I bought my first motor launch when they made me head of the Southern England, but it was a pathetic, paltry little thing. Then, about a year ago, I decided to trade it in for a younger model. Not bad for a guy with a 2-2 from Birkbeck, hey?"

Hand crafted in Milan, Roger's boat was sleek and narrow with a light tan finish. It was the kind of machine that made a man want to reach out and touch, long before he really ought to. The hull had been painted in the deepest possible blue and as far as Crispin could make out, it had yet to acquire a single scratch. Given Roger's obsession with money markets, it was hard to imagine he had a lot of experience on the water.

Wrong! In a matter of seconds the engines were frantic and the boys were speeding due west. Dignified on Crispin's immediate left, Roger gazed into the middle distance and started to quote Grahame.

"My dear, Crispin, *there is nothing, absolutely nothing like messing about on the river.*"

Crispin couldn't actually remember what Roger had studied at University, but it was unlikely to be literature for the under 12s. Sensing that he had being cast as the hesitant Mole to Roger's debonair Rat, he decided not to comment. Besides, Crispin was more than willing to distract himself with the view from the helm. Spinning around, he saw the Millennium Dome and a river that seemed to veer to the left as it rolled out towards the sea. In the days of the Bard – Crispin knew – the Thames would have been even broader here, spilling its banks over untamed marshland to the South.

But for Roger, this place was his back yard and Crispin felt the need to make small talk.

"I mean, what's it like living in this sort of area? Is there a problem with crime?"

Roger shook his head.

"What about flooding? Do you worry about that?" asked Crispin. "This far down stream?"

"We're not going to get wet here, mate!" shouted Roger, his cheeks already damp with the freshwater spray. "There's a million pound flood barrier behind us. If it swamps your Morgan, I'll want my bloody taxes back!"

It seemed to Crispin that the flood barrier cost a lot more than a million pounds, but he wasn't here to argue. The river was vast now with rigid borders and they need only follow its arching path if they wanted to reach the Globe. Here on the open deck of an Italian speedboat, Crispin had never felt so close to the elements and yet – at the same time – he had never felt so tightly hemmed in. How on Earth could he feel so threatened by the wild, here in the very centre of this vast metropolis?

Distant to the south, the cranes of a lost city rose up from dark concrete and Crispin drew breath as they rushed by.

Relaxed besides the wheel, Roger attempted to justify his outlay.

"I find travel by motor launch so much simpler than car. What with the congestion charge and all the parking fines one finds on the roads these days."

But Crispin wasn't listening. The river itself had seized his attention and in a world where a man's view is forever disturbed by clutter, the uninterrupted lines of sight that stem from open water were blowing his mind. First, came the bars and jetties of the 19th century. Then, the looming battlements of Tower Bridge. A short while later, he saw a stronghold that had been built by the Duke of Normandy. Out here on the river, the Sun itself seemed brighter and

Crispin would have been happy to stay here all day and skip the bit with the diaries completely, but Roger had other ideas.

"So, how much do you think it would be worth?" he asked. "If you're right and they're really in this box?"

Crispin shrugged like he hadn't a clue and Roger didn't push it, slowing very gently as they approached the next Bridge. Their speed changed with the sound of the engine and for the best part of ten seconds, the vessel was enshrined by gleaming brick. Then, suddenly, the arches vanished and the sun returned to greet them. An impressive white hexagon had appeared on the south bank, strangely out of place amidst the steel and concrete of the modern age. The story of this theatre was – Crispin knew – one of the more cringe worthy anecdotes in 20th Century history. In a country that never ceased to tire of its greatest playwright, support for the project had been thin on the ground, and it took the drive of the American film Producer - Sam Wanamaker - to get the thing finished.

As soon as it opened, the replica theatre was hailed as a masterpiece and all kinds of people came out of the woodwork to say what a great idea it was. In time, it even inspired a kind of living archaeology, with modern day directors competing to deliver their plot lines from the limits of a Tudor stage.

"What about this Lucy character?" asked Roger, adjusting the wheel as they approached the pontoon. "I mean, have you got her down in your address book under L?" Crispin had. "You see, that's a real mistake. You really need to think about an alpha numeric coding system for your women. I've had one for a year or so and it's really changed my life. If I can find the App, I can send you the link."

The embankment beckoned and Crispin ran to the damp stone staircase that would take them to the Globe. Slipping on the very first stone, he managed to dunk one foot in the river and by the time he regained his balance, the cotton was cold and soaked as high as the knee. This was the kind of cock up that was bound to raise a laugh from Roger, but the theatre was almost upon them, and Crispin was able to redirect their conversation with the issue of tickets.

Shakespeare isn't always a sell out and there were more than enough seats on the door. Concerned that Roger might do a runner, Crispin paid for the pair of them with his credit card and, a few minutes later, they were standing at the back, waiting for it all to get going. Over to Crispin's right, another question had entered Roger's head.

"Did Shakespeare write *Hamlet* too?"

"*SSShhhhhh!*"

Crispin suggested that he had and Roger replied in kind. "A 2-2." he conceded, sotto voce. "Management and Economics."

"*Sssshhhh!*"

But there was more going on here than stage craft. Unbeknown to the boys, they were now sharing this theatre with an interested third party. Wiser and more accomplished than all of his enemies, Kranz was barely visible on the far right of the crowd. There was little sign of rain, but rain can harass the English at any time of the day or night and it seemed entirely reasonable for Kranz to stand here with his hood up and an umbrella on standby. Whatever, Crispin's attention was fixed on the stage, where young Lucy would surely soon appear. Silent in the aisles, Arthur Kranz turned very briefly to his left. The boys were in position and were here to serve his cause.

The action, when it came, was sudden and intense. The people of Rome are in awe of Caesar and rejoice in his victory over Pompey, but the people are fickle too. Whilst the proles prepare to holiday, the public officials attempt to put them down. In days gone by, the mid-ranking official, Flavius, could guess a man's status from his dress sense, but in these strange and altered times, such markers have vanished and the world is out of control. Support for the ruling class has splintered and no one can predict how the masses will react. There is a looming danger here too, one that Roger completely failed to pick up on, but that an Elizabethan audience would – presumably – have grasped immediately.

Access wise, Crispin and Roger were secure. They had purchased tickets on the door but - as Crispin well knew - this was very much a modern tradition. Four hundred years ago, they would have had teenage boys wandering around the place with a hat, demanding a penny from everyone upright in the yard. Never mind that the actors were already talking. Access was free and nobody had to pay if they weren't thoroughly thrilled. Shakespeare would have had no quarrel with the opening panorama shot of your average Hollywood blockbuster. If you can't grab these people early on, how do you expect to get your hands on their cash?

Meanwhile, back in the open air theatre, Caesar was talking about himself in the third person:

"Danger knows full well
That Caesar is more dangerous than he:
We are two lions littered in one day,
And I the elder and more terrible."

Chapter 24

It was almost done. The body of Brutus had been laid out and Mark Anthony – the playboy soldier – offered this eulogy for a fallen foe.

> *"His life was gentle; and the elements*
> *So mixed in him, that Nature might stand up*
> *And say to all the world, this was a man!"*

This most stageable of plays had drawn to a close and Roger felt the need to comment.

"That had better not be the First Act!"

It wasn't the First Act and the man with a 2-2 in Management and Economics was visibly relieved. More to the point, he had a burning desire for booze. By sheer luck, they were well within striking distance of one of his favourite haunts and Roger knew a short cut. As far as Crispin could tell, this whole place had been assembled under some huge Victorian railway arch and cordoned off with a smoked glass window. When the first train rolled overhead, it would – presumably – put an end to all conversation but Roger wasn't worried about this, demanding two pints more or less as soon as he walked through the door. The bar girls seemed to know him and the beer, when it came, was iced and amber and white on the top. Swilling the stuff down with real gusto, Crispin described his ill timed approach to Tom's veranda. Roger asked how much footage he'd managed to capture on the smart phone and the doctor was forced to offer two excuses where one would have done.

"It was a difficult angle. I couldn't let go of the ivy."

"Well, we could go back together. I could put it on You Tube."

"Yes, but it wouldn't be so good. If he wasn't with the girl."

"Oh, that doesn't matter. I betcha if we climbed in every night for a week, he'd be at it at least once."

Emboldened by the thing with the ivy, Roger decided to make a move on the barmaid. What came next was so dreadful that Crispin could barely bring himself to watch, but Roger was completely undefeated, marching along with the same filthy grin on his face and snatching another drink from the other barmaid.

And then, without warning, there was music. Ten feet behind them, a man in a dinner jacket had sat down beside an upright piano. His was a dazzling performance in an offbeat joint where the near total absence of soft furnishing gave a strange metallic thrill to every note. It occurred to Crispin that our time in this world is short and that these last few days had been so crammed with thrills and spills that the issue of Kranz and the stolen documents barely mattered.

Seconds later, Lucy Bernstein arrived in person and the entire bar came to a standstill.

There wasn't a bang. There wasn't any flying shrapnel or flames that lapped around the door, but to the observant amongst them, the mood was different. All across the room, men abandoned their own girls and undressed her with their eyes. If anything, this was even more striking than the night when she saved Crispin from a miniature uprising in the Dog and Duck. In his next life, Crispin would come back as a sheer blonde from the Midwest. Never again would he find himself sidelined by the wider world. Never again would he park in a corner or bargain with his peers for a slice of their lives. Nor would he want for social contact, evening dinner dates or casual small talk. No matter how long it took to colour that hair, it would be worth it.

Crispin introduced her to Roger and Roger told Lucy about his boat, his collection of handmade sports jackets and his net income for a typical month.

"I say typical," he added. "Obviously, it can be much more than that."

As far as the diaries went, Lucy was doubting but not unsupportive. In any case, the effort required to prove Crispin wrong was really quite minor. Not only had Lucy driven down from Scotland in the RSC lorry, she had actually watched them unload the contents at the Globe. All they needed to do now was walk into the store room beneath the stage and prise open the offending boxes. Having established that the boxes were empty, they could return to the pub.

Brilliant! Crispin was in complete agreement. If the diaries were somewhere else, he could live with it. At least he would have had a go.

The actress produced the key to the stage door and placed it on the bar. She knew how long it took for the stage hands to lock up the theatre and she knew how long it would take to order another round.

Seeing his chance, Roger began to tell her about the special brewing process that was used to make their drinks. It could only be done in Belgium and Roger had actually visited the brewery during a weekend trip to Brussels. Ever since then, whenever he wanted to get rat-faced in South London, he always came to this exact same spot, sometimes speaking with a Flemish accent whilst he ordered the first round.

An hour or so later, three unlikely looking art thieves returned to the Globe as a group. The storeroom was crammed with discarded Roman armour and half-opened boxes and within a matter of seconds, Crispin and Roger were tearing through each of them in turn.

Relaxed by an open doorway, Lucy proved a dab hand at *sarcasm*: "Don't suppose either of you guys would be interested in having a delve there."

But the boys weren't listening. Roger had seen something that looked like a book. "It's here," he said, annoying Crispin by finding it first. "This is it."

Crispin raised his smart phone and tried to use the screen as a light source. The nearest box was still emblazoned with the letters RSC119, although this sequence meant nothing to them. Arthur had stuffed his priceless treasure beneath the props and as fate might have it, no one had opened this box since the Fringe.

For the second time this summer, a previously unknown General Practitioner from Stratford had just set hands on the lost diaries of William Shakespeare, and this time it felt better than the first. A few steps behind them, Lucy said something pertinent. Were any of these pages legible?

"Barely," whispered Crispin. "It's all squiggles."

"It could say anything with that handwriting!"

It was an exchange that might have gone on for longer but for the arrival of a new and unexpected guest, fully equipped with a large black handgun and a carefully folded bag.

"Bad luck!" said Winston, dropping the bag and raising the gun. "You guys were gonna be famous all over again."

Crispin looked directly at the long black barrel and started to see it end on. Since the earliest days of childhood, he had been aided and abetted by his father's brother and Crispin felt a pang of guilt that every penny that Jack had ever spent on him was about to be thrown away. Worse than that, he had just dragged a couple of total innocents into the firing line.

But there was hope. There were a great many people in South London and the weapon lacked a silencer. The new arrival was anything but a walk-in thief and it seemed unlikely that Winston would open fire in this location.

"So, who's this geyser?" asked Roger, buoyant, like he wanted to get them all shot.

"Winston's the name. 'Them books is my game," said Winston, stumbling a bit with his delivery. And then he waved the gun some more and tried to sound friendly: "I think I can relieve you of these items."

Winston stepped forward and began to throw the books into his bag. Seconds later, he was hauling the thing around like Santa Claus and backing off towards the door. That same door slammed very loudly and the room beneath the Globe became possessed by a new and unintended silence. Roger asked if the gun was likely to have been loaded. Crispin said that it was and Lucy – who already knew this – let him down badly by starting to jibber.

"*You said it was just a few books!*"

A minute or so passed by and they decided to approach the door as a group. Nudging the thing open with one foot, Crispin looked out at an empty street.

"He could be anywhere!" yelled Lucy, furious in the doorway. "You guys 'ell never find him!"

But Lucy was wrong. Winston's strategy was plain to see and against all expectations, Roger was about to rise to the occasion. "Come along, young Crispin!" he shouted. "Let's get after him."

"Where did he go?"

"Elementary, my dear Watson. It's all in the *hem line*."

Chapter 25

And so it was! Soaking one leg in the River Thames isn't an easy thing to do, but Winston had done it anyway, slipping on the exact same step that had previously scuppered Crispin. If he'd come here by boat, then it was reasonable to suppose he would be leaving by boat too, and when the boys arrived at the black Pontoon, they could actually see Winston's vessel, darting under the first road bridge and storming due east.

Scalded by their earlier defeat, Crispin and Roger jumped into Roger's speed machine and prepared to cast off.

"What shall *I* do?" Shouted Lucy, loudly and with no intention of joining them.

"Oh, don't worry about us!" cried Crispin. "We'll call you!"

Crispin was in a hurry, but Roger wasn't. Traversing the first bridge at a steady pace, the business and economics graduate decided to play it safe until they were well clear of the brickwork. Then, suddenly, they were out onto open water and picking up speed. Swerving wildly to port, Roger ripped past a well known Norman fortress and raced towards Tower Bridge. Winston's boat was lively, but it was small and underpowered and over a race of some distance, Roger was confident they could catch up.

The spray, the booze, the wind in their face, all of these things were there to distract them from those same life changing risks they had already countenanced, and the rest of their day might have turned out a lot better if it hadn't been for a pugnacious burst of gunfire from the boat up ahead. The very first round smashed into Roger's hull and Crispin was soon horrified by the thought of the repair bill.

"It may be time to call the police!" shouted Roger, calm and collected, like Gregory Peck in *12 O'Clock High*.

Roger brought his phone to one ear, only to watch it shatter as a second missile hit its mark. Containing his fear, Roger sought solace in the logic of mass production.

"It's alright," he said, dropping the damaged handset. "They make millions of these! There's a factory."

There was indeed a factory, but it wasn't here and it wasn't being shot at under Tower Bridge. A slither of touch sensitive plastic had stabbed Roger in the face and Crispin saw blood streak down from the eyebrow. More bullets streamed in and the starboard motor began to moan. Roger turned around and saw thick black smoke. It was a major setback, but the second engine was still working and they were able to return to the Marina at low revs.

Escaping the boat with a mighty bound, Crispin marvelled at the sheer speed with which his luck could change in these adventures. He had survived another encounter with the mythical figure of Kranz, but - as with his race through the meadow - it was the people around him who were taking the flak.

The blood on Roger's face had dried in the slip stream and there was nothing else coming out. Convinced that he could fix this and anything else on this planet, Crispin broke off to retrieve his brown leather bag from his overpriced, over-engineered, English sports car. Back in Roger's apartment, he opened a tiny adhesive dressing and pressed it very neatly onto Roger's brow.

Roger ran to the mirror to check his new look. His look was good. Getting shot at on the Thames was the most exciting thing that had happened to him since the second year summer ball and the square sticky dressing had done a lot to enhance his image.

"If that bar maid had seen me like this, I think I could have shagged her!"

But by now, it really was time to call the police. Searching for the nearest landline, The boys were rudely interrupted when the door burst open and a bearded American arrived in the hallway, fully equipped with a gratuitously large handgun and bullish henchmen. Having been humiliated in Scotland, Kranz was in no mood to accept defeat here.

A few miles to the West, a second body of men were lingering by the Globe, watching from a distance and thinking about their fee. Innocent in their gaze, Lucy was being indecisive. Retreating to her dressing room, she was soon evicted by the cleaners and left in the narrow alleyway that skirted the building. Alarmed and confused, she walked back to the jetty and looked out across the Thames.

What had happened to Roger and Crispin? Why hadn't she received a call or a text? In the thick of it, Lucy even felt a wave of contempt for the pair of them. How dumb did these kids have to be, to chase an armed man in a boat? When they themselves had no weapons and no experience of violence or the criminal underworld?

Some people have a low threshold for calling the police. Lucy wasn't one of them, but on this occasion, she had little choice. Reaching for her phone, she froze very suddenly as cold black metal pressed against her spine.

Chapter 26

In the Northern Hemisphere, the prevailing wind direction is from the west and for this reason, every major city in Europe has placed its poor in the east. London was no exception and it was the East of the city that became the home for the docks and the unskilled labour that served them.

But nothing lasts forever and by the early 1980s, the docks were pretty much done for. After a brief period of stagnation, a group of farsighted business men moved in and bought up the entire region for a pittance. Overnight, Docklands became the most sought after property market in Europe and every warehouse in sight was marked for redevelopment.

It is a process that goes on to this day and one of the last derelict buildings on the water front was now home to Kranz and his men. Disciplined to the last, Kranz's men were rounding up their kit and shifting it over to their hire cars. At the bottom of a dark and filthy basement, two prisoners had been tied to the floor.

Staring at the walls, Crispin felt his blood begin to chill. Some distance to their West of this building, an immense gateway had been closed and lowered into the water. The Thames is a tidal river and its level was rising with the sea.

Whatever happened next, Lucy wouldn't be here to see it. Kranz had taken an executive decision and she was to be kept outside where her newly appointed minder, Gary, would watch from a distance and pretend not to lech. Gary's right hand was deep inside his bulging ski jacket and the outline of a gun was difficult to ignore.

The rear of the warehouse looked out onto an uneven field of weeds and low grade rubble. Further away and beyond the building, Lucy saw a narrow road. Since their arrival, some twenty minutes ago, not a single vehicle had passed them by. This was a place where no one would hear her scream, although it was not inconceivable that a shot from a gun might draw attention.

She remembered a discourse she had once received from a pre-pubescent girl in New York. Barely into her teens, the girl had been black or African-American or whatever other word was in vogue for some kid on the street, but in Lucy's mind she was really only a child. The pair of them had been standing on the unvarnished floorboards of a penthouse apartment in the Bronx. High as a kite and strangely serene, her lecture went like this:

Don't let them get you on the floor. Don't let them get you indoors and wherever they take you, don't let them get you on the floor. They can only kill you once and from their own perspective, the only thing more important than killing you, is getting away with it.

Arthur approached from the south, tall and stone-faced in the same Khaki Trench Coat he'd unwrapped by a canal near Stratford. And amidst the impending horror of her predicament, it occurred to Lucy that there was something strangely dignified about his stance. Even serene.

This was the fourth and final act. If there was a curtain in these God forsaken islands, then it was almost upon them and Arthur wouldn't be here for the encore.

"The big question," he asked, "is where will you be?"

Where would she be? Lucy didn't give him an answer, but Kranz seemed to find one on her face.

"With or without." With and it wouldn't be easy. They were heading for another world and when they got there, there wouldn't be much in the way of creature comforts.

Just as Arthur began to do concern, Lucy began to speak. She spoke of their shared values, of their first meeting in a sacred place and the conversation that came forthwith.

Did Arthur remember that?

He did. The street, the taxi, the middle part of the afternoon. He remembered all of it. Even the rules. He remembered telling her that there wouldn't be any.

Arthur turned around and moved to kiss her, a loud and unexpected act of catharsis that caught the onlookers unawares. For her part, the girl seemed neutral, accepting but barely giving back.

There was a van behind the warehouse and it was there to steal her away. A few months ago, there had been talk of Chicago, then this Stratford thing came up. Late morning, she had been someone in The Globe and by this time tomorrow, she would be lying in a strange and foreign land.

The van had a rough, basic interior and in a way – for Lucy – it was a form of release. No need to worry about angry directors. No need to worry about written contracts or unwashed linen. She need never stoop so low. 'Never again.

They slammed the doors. She was on her way but for Arthur, there was one more task to perform. Descending a dark staircase, Arthur entered the ancient basement where he came across his men, the last vestiges of his adventures in England and his principal rival in life.

Taking up position behind his captives, Arthur started to talk about culture. 'A common culture. Some time ago, Arthur had met one of Crispin's compatriots in New York. "Weird little guy by the name of Winnie. 'Lives in a Manhattan these days. I think they've got him in a glass box."

"Ah yes!" said Crispin, jesting from what was likely to be his death bed. "Our greatest living export."

Arthur kinked his neck and did his best to look Crispin in the eye.

"And you know, I thought about you guys and I thought, these Brits have got a *huge* problem. Your *history*. There's just *too much* of it. And as a God-faring American, I feel strongly that I should help with the act of redistribution!"

Arthur broke into a vast and largely unconvincing smile. Seconds later, he turned to leave and Crispin felt the need to shout.

"*Kranz!* This is a civilised country! There are police! Courts!"

But the Great Arthur Kranz was unmoved. "Are you telling me you wouldn't have done the same? Surely you, of all people, can see what these books represent!"

Barring his imminent goodbye to Roger, this was likely to be Crispin's last conversation. There had been something on his mind for some time now and he wanted to clear it up.

"What does it say in them?"

"A few sonnets, a spare play or two. Nothing to write home about."

"*Bastard!*"

"Incidentally, your lodger will be leaving with me. I've got her down for a one-way trip across the Baltic."

This didn't sound very promising either, but Roger was thinking about something else.

"What about us?"

"Sorry, Roger!" said Arthur, trying his hand at RP. "The tide waits for no man."

"They built a barrage for that kind of thing!" shouted Roger. "It won a design award."

"Too bad we're downstream." Called Arthur, stepping back into the darkness and leaving them both to die.

Chapter 27

Whilst all this was happening, the rest of London was about to defend itself against the sea. As was the norm in this situation, this task had been delegated to a small group of engineers in the Barrage Control room.

Upstream and to the west of this barrier, the city would be shielded by a series of massive steel gates. But this kind of approach comes at a price. East of the barrage, water levels would climb very rapidly and long before they reached their peak, Crispin and Roger would be dead.

Having escaped to the surface, Arthur Kranz was tying up loose ends. His new boys were standing around for payment and he had to dispose of them fast. Receiving their money in haste, they drifted away on foot. Kranz took comfort from the fact that they barely understood what he'd stolen. That been said, they hadn't signed up for a share of the profits either and with a deal like that, betrayal in itself would be a zero risk game.

Kranz needed to get out of here now.

Down in the cellar, Al was almost ready to go. With the bulk of his kit already packed, his thoughts turned to a handsome doctor's bag on the floor. Al picked it up, tore the thing open and split the contents onto his feet.

Petrified on the dank concrete, Roger made one last bid for freedom.

"Look," he shouted, "let's look at this from a financial perspective. How much is he paying you and have you seen my bank statement?"

Neither man appeared to hear.

"Because I could pay the pair of you off right now. 'Get you two tickets to a very nice place in Rio. Al, have you ever been to Rio?"

Al - who might well have been to Rio - decided to ignore this one too. Better than that, he decided to stand in the doorway and cough, very loudly. One step closer to his maker, Crispin tried a different line.

"Al?" he hissed. "Al? That wheeze still playing you up?"

Al's body seemed to creak – very slightly – in mid-step and Crispin ran straight to the issue of chest pain. In particular, the kind of stabbing, retrosternal pain that might well be felt on exertion.

"I mean," he continued, "what about heavy lifting? Does that make it worse?"

Al reached into his breast pocket and stroked his inhaler.

"This stuff will see me through, Doctor Shakespeare. You just keep on dying—"

"Have you always had that pallor in your eyes?"

"Pallor?" scowled the American. Then, "Oh, you don't scare me!"

Eager to sound helpful, Winston confided in his victims. "He's had that asthma longer than my angina!"

"*Angina?* Christ, Winston! At *your* age? I had to attend an autopsy on a guy with angina, the other day. It was an absolutely dreadful thing! Al, have you ever had one of those ECGs? Where they stick all those wires on your chest? In fact, Al, if you don't mind me asking…?"

Al dropped his cargo and shifted both hands to his hips. He was, Roger feared, about to stamp on Crispin's face.

"*What* don't I mind you asking?"

"Are you having problems, sustaining your *erections*? These days?"

The man with the long term wheeze fell silent.

"You don't get back pain too do you?" asked Crispin. "Because I had some ECG kit in my bag over there. I'd hate to see you escape the country without having your ticker checked. What use is a payoff then?"

"What use is a payoff then?" echoed Roger, sodden as high as his waist.

Winston moved to release Crispin. Al agreed to lie down on a bench whilst Crispin rummaged through the contents of his bag and recovered his portable ECG machine from the mess. Seconds later, the doctor stuck a few electrodes to the man's chest and coaxed his machine into life.

A couple of wavy lines ran across the screen and Crispin spoke with real gravitas: "It's not good," he announced. "Al, when did you last see your doctor in the States?"

America is sometimes portrayed as a land of opportunity, but the barrier that is wealth had long been obvious to Al.

"Back in the States?" he whimpered. "Back in the States, we couldn't afford no doctor!"

"You see," said Crispin, trying his hand at *empathy*, "on the National Health Service, this sort of thing would be free."

"Free at the point of access," quirked Roger, about five octaves too high.

"That's true, Al," said Winston. "Over here, you don't have to pay money for this kind of thing."

"Didn't your mother have a doctor?" asked Crispin, being careful to place more emphasis on the word *mother* than doctor.

"Oh Jes! Doc!" wailed Winston. "Don't ask him about his mother!"

But he already had.

"*My mother*!" Al exclaimed, "Christ! Doc! Let me tell you about my mother!"

Crispin produced a small gas cylinder and thoughtfully applied a plastic mask over Al's mouth.

"Keep telling me about your mother, whilst you inhale on this stuff."

Turning to Winston, Crispin pointed to the mask. "You just press on there mate, that's your job."

Winston pressed on there and Crispin snapped open a glass vial and used it to fill a 5ml syringe. By now, the cockney was totally gripped.

"How did you know he had back pain?" he said, not bothering to look up.

"There's only one thing more common than back pain, mate."

"What's that?" asked Winston, wincing a bit whilst Crispin stabbed him in the thigh.

"Erectile dysfunction!"

Winston's mouth opened very widely, but before he had time to speak, he was falling to the ground. Snatching the pistol from Winston's pocket, Crispin checked the firing mechanism. The firing mechanism was good. Seconds later, the gas sapped the last of Al's strength and the keys to Roger's chains clanged loudly against the concrete.

Time to get up and run.

The warehouse was separated from the rest of the city by about fifty yards of scraggy grassland and the boys traversed it with manic haste. A few seconds later, they made it to a narrow winding lane where they came across the only listed building in the region: a small red telephone box that had seen better days. Crispin flung open the cast iron door and made a spot diagnosis: *torn electrical cable*. Some three months ago, a thoughtful teenager had absconded with the handset. In fact, time had not been kind to this edifice at all. Practically all the windows were broken and most of the red paint was flaking off. Apart from that it was fine.

Roger, who had fallen behind a bit, collided with the box. "Can't believe how you managed to turn that around!" he gasped, his brain still trapped in the cellar. It was looking grim, but their luck was about to change. After an hour or so of virtually no traffic, a single black cab charged around the corner and Roger flagged it down.

Their driver was bored, grey and grateful for the gig.

"Where to, Governor?"

"Docklands!" shouted Crispin, much too loudly. "Docklands City Airport!"

Whilst Docklands was a great location for a business district, the docks of the 19th century had never been particularly well connected to the rest of the city and when the architects of the 1980s were planning the new East End, they quickly commissioned a new public transport system with a simple title: "The Docklands Light Railway". In time, a strip of land beside the river would be converted into a regional airport and the dock lands departure lounge has been a byword for overcrowding ever since. But airports do a lot more than carry people. At least half of their income stems from freight and this very evening, Kranz and his team were planning to escape the British Isles in a twin engined turboprop of their own.

Two of his men had stayed behind in the warehouse and were under strict instructions to hold their position until Roger and Crispin were dead. Meanwhile, Arthur and Gary had gathered in one of the smaller hangers at the airport and were standing by to board their plane. Although their mission was far from over, there was a mounting sense of excitement and their nondescript twin engine turbo prop was fuelled and ready for take-off. Arthur's last minute passenger lacked any kind of travel documents, but where this plane was going, they wouldn't be asked for visas.

Some distance from the airfield, Crispin was concerned about traffic flow, his concern here being that there wasn't any. As with every other piece of infrastructure in this region, this road had been congested to the point of madness from the day it first opened and it might have been easier to walk. Furious on the back seat, Roger had discovered a massive stain on his shirt. Given that he had been very nearly drowned in the river, this wasn't as shocking as it might have been, but Roger decided to moan about it anyway. "*Don't* call the police?" he started. "What if they put us on TV? I have a solid reputation for sartorial elegance! Then what?"

Glancing up through the meshwork ahead of them, Crispin caught on to a crisis in the making. Their driver was a long standing opponent of the 1967 Sexual Offences Act and Roger was rubbing him up the wrong way.

"Hey!" shouted Roger. "Let's be clear about something else! I have not and never will have erectile dysfunction!"

The vehicle came to a screaming halt and the man behind the wheel decided to go mental. "Right! That's it! There's only *one* rule in this cab! No junkies, no suicide bombers and no arse bandits!" Roger protested in the obscene, but the cabbie had only just started. "I blame that flower power crap! That and that Mick – bleed - in' - Jagger music!"

Through the left window, Crispin saw an important road sign: LONDON CITY AIRPORT 1 MILE

Having recovered his strength in the back seat, he felt he could make it to the perimeter fence without coming up for air.

Egressing in haste, Crispin left Roger to the cabbie and started to run.

Chapter 28

Over in the airport, Arthur's turboprop was dormant in the hanger. Their luggage was already on board, but the all important books were still beside his feet. To Gary, they were completely worthless, his perfect booty. To Arthur, they were treasure beyond description. Under guard at the rear of the aircraft, Lucy was more concerned with her own survival.

"It's not British Airways."

Arthur's response was calm and self-assured. "They're a little too keen on security."

But Arthur had more on his mind than Lucy. His people in the warehouse were failing to respond and the hour of their departure was fast approaching.

Arthur turned to Gary and asked him to put out another call. *Where the hell are you?* Or words to that extent. Gary did as he was told and once again, Al failed to respond. Conscious of the mounting sense of panic, Lucy stepped a little closer to the turboprop and peered in through a tiny portal.

This wasn't a passenger aircraft. Half a dozen seats folded down behind the cockpit. Behind that, there was only empty space and then a second, giant beak of an exit that was meant to receive a larger cargo.

Nodding towards the aircraft, Gary made reference to the onboard ladies' room, the reference being that there wasn't one.

"Well then," said Lucy. "I better go now."

Arthur watched her recede and made no comment. Waiting by the fuselage, he pressed on 'call' all over again, and barked another batch of orders through his phone.

No answer. This was it. They were going to have to leave. *Now*.

Lucy didn't look back and Gary trailed her like an automaton, stopping just short of the women's toilets. Moving inside, Lucy counted her blessings in borderline silence. Pay phones were an endangered species in modern Britain, but Lucy had found one anyway and this one was actually intact.

And it was at precisely this point that Crispin decided to appear. Unseen and flustered, he glanced round the edge of the fire door and noted Kranz and his very pragmatic turboprop. Seeing Gary by the toilet door, Crispin moved for cover and tried to control his breathing.

Still hidden besides a sink, Lucy tapped a mechanical keyboard and began to whitter in code: "9-1-1. Call 9-1-1."

Nothing happened and she typed it all again, scathing with the handset whilst the speaker rattled in her ear. "*Come on, come on, come on!*" It was a prayer that brought an unexpected response. For the second time in one day, the barrel of a gun was crushed against her spine.

"In this country," came a cruel Northern voice, "the number to call is 999."

It would be misleading to suggest that Lucy was some kind of novice in the land of violence because she wasn't. There has always been a powerful link between thuggery and glamour and she had dealt with these people before. Like Crispin before her, she noted that the handgun carried no silencer. Discharging a weapon in an airport was bound to draw attention and the odds were stacked towards survival.

A few yards short of the aircraft, she felt the need to speak. "Arthur!"

Where were they going?

But Arthur's mind was heading elsewhere. If Winston and Al weren't reacting, it was likely that something had happened and if something had happened, then the police might be here at any moment.

Over on the turboprop, their pilot was already in position. Adjusting his lip mike, they heard him speak to the control tower:

"Victor Nine Zero Five. Victor Nine Zero Five. Are you receiving me?"

They couldn't afford to wait any longer and Arthur gave the order to climb on board. Seconds later, hatches were slamming and the port side engine burst into life.

Glancing down towards his feet, Arthur Kranz checked the position of a single wooden box. The box was secure and present. There might have been more comfort for him in holding the thing in flight, but the books were too numerous and too heavy. A little further away, he could see his trusty leather suitcase, hooked to the wall and ready for action. For as far back as he could remember, that thing had followed him through all of his adventures. In the arrivals lounge of your average airport it's sheer mundaneness seemed to boost his confidence and it remained the only visible connection to the Princeton of his youth

What was there left to do now? Worry about interception in the air? Running out of fuel?

Tightening the straps around his shoulders, Kranz closed his eyes and tried to list every detail he had ever given to Al. Would the police be able to follow them? Not immediately, but there was enough in Al's head to make things difficult for Kranz and he wished he hadn't put it there.

This was as good a time as any for Crispin to change position. Stepping out from the sidelines, he dashed to the rear of the aircraft and secured himself in the hold, just as the cargo bay doors closed behind him.

The engines were getting louder, but the aircraft had yet to move. Crispin started to worry that he had been rumbled and that their journey might never begin. Reaching into his pocket, he fingered the handgun he had taken from Al. Crispin had fired a similar weapon in the TA, killing a few cardboard cutouts along the way He drew the gun closer to his face and felt the cold metal press against his skin.

Could he fire it here? Today?

Then, suddenly, there was movement, hesitant for the first thirty seconds and then much faster as the aircraft approached the runway. If Crispin was going to act, he was going to have to do it now. Inching towards the hatch, he shook the handle to the next compartment. Nothing happened and new wave of anguish poured out across his soul. Prior to this moment, he had been calm, but the adrenaline was getting the better of him and he could feel the terror in his hands. Desperate for a secondary mechanism of release, Crispin ran his fingers along the edges of the hatch and found nothing.

Too late! The aircraft charged down the runway and sprang up into the sky. Lacking both a chair and a safety belt, Crispin pressed his hands against the walls for balance and tried not to scream.

How the hell was he going to get out of this one?

Outside and across the city, Kranz's aircraft was just another siren in the clouds, one more mid-sized cargo flight, soaring out across the Thames. There was no word from the control tower and no sign of pursuit.

Lucy glanced out of the window and grasped her situation in depth. The Manhattan-like towers of Canary Wharf were a tiny model village, their blunted summits punching briefly through the clouds. This was more than a good take-off. This was getting away with it.

She turned to Kranz and watched him smile. She made an effort to smile back, but on this occasion, her temperament failed her and the best she could offer was a desperate grimace.

Time for questions: "Arthur! Where are we going?"

But Arthur was falling back on their past. "How would Oscar Wilde have put it?" he asked her. "To reject one suitor is unfortunate. To reject two seems careless."

"Are you still getting off on that shit? What are you going to do with him?"

Arthur moved one hand, as if to draw his gun and Lucy failed to react. After a few seconds, he let it slip, meaning what? Meaning there would be time later?

But Arthur Kranz wasn't the only man with a gun. Twenty feet behind them, Crispin finally forced open the doorway to the main compartment. The release - when it came - was much more abrupt than he had planned for and the scene that awaited him, more than surreal.

"Arthur!" he shouted, concerned as he did so that his voice might be lost in the background noise.

Glancing at each of the players in turn, the American raised a fresh smile and shouted back: "Doctor Shakespeare? Where'd you learn to use that thing?"

"The TA!"

"The *Territorial Army*?" This time, the laughter was real. "What part of killing did they teach you last week?"

"Pulling the trigger!"

Arthur had a point. Crispin wasn't a natural born killer and this kind of work was way outside his comfort zone. The city was far behind them and the aircraft was fast approaching the sea. Though their location remained irrelevant, Crispin felt an overwhelming urge to turn to this left and check the tiny portal by the door.

Arthur shouted something else.

"What about the pilot? Are you going to kill him too? Me, my crew, the pilot?"

"I can land this thing on my own!" Called Crispin.

This was an exaggeration. Some years ago, Crispin had forked out for five flying lessons in Gloucestershire, but finally jacked it in on the grounds of cost.

Over in the corner, Arthur's boy, Gary, was about to show initiative. Slowly, very slowly, he moved one hand towards his gun. Having secured the thing beneath his own straps, he hadn't expected to use it during flight. Several feet ahead of him, an anxious pilot glanced over his shoulder, his face barely visible in the slit like corridor that reversed from the cockpit.

Crispin jerked his pistol towards the pilot and was about to go loud when Gary seized his chance. Changing his aim, Crispin squeezed the trigger and felt his weapon kick. Gary fell flail and for an instant, the collective squeal from his audience seemed to drown out the engines. It was a dramatic and decisive action that took them all by surprise, no one more so than Crispin. But for Arthur, it was the beginning of something else. The game was nearly up. He could fight here or succumb to British Justice. As Crispin should have known by now, fighting came much easier to Arthur than defeat. Grabbing some kind of lever on the wall, Arthur threw open the cargo bay door in the centre of the fuselage and all hell broke loose.

There was a fantastic rush of air and a rut of screaming. Ahead of Crispin, the pilot had formulated an escape manoeuvre of his own and decided to fling them all left with a sudden shift to the controls. Crispin lost his balance but landed on both feet and his left hand, with the gun secure in his right. In so far as he was distracted, the manoeuvre had worked but Gary's pistol, already loose against his boots, was rolling – impulsively – towards the yawning gap in the fuselage. Seconds later, it was on its way to the sea.

Kranz's entire team had just disarmed themselves and before Crispin could stand upright, Kranz had forced open a compartment on the wall and gotten himself a flare gun. He might have fired the thing on impulse, but some kind of scuffle exploded around him and in a strange flurry of limbs, nothing came Crispin's way. Later, he would try to convince himself that it was Lucy that had intervened though he would never be certain. Whatever, Arthur lost his aim and the flash, when it came, was red and sudden and fizzing in a suitcase to their rear.

Maybe it was fitting. Al and Winston had, after all, desecrated Crispin's bag in the warehouse. But by now the aircraft had developed a mind of its own, lurching to starboard and scaring the shit out of all of them. Lucy made an effort to steady herself on the fuselage and failed miserably, skidding towards the middle of the hold and colliding bodily with the all important box. The box didn't like it very much either and to Crispin's undisguised horror, a mass of paperwork broke loose and slipped out towards the clouds.

The clouds vanished and Crispin saw open water through the hatch. Something without price had been lost forever. Worse still, he had lost his footing again and was likely to die in the same ocean. Scared senseless by the thought of it, Crispin let go of his handgun and reached out to save himself, just as Arthur managed to re-load.

It was time for action. Crispin jumped across the open cargo bay doors and landed on Arthur Kranz. The man's head struck the wall and his fingers twitched in the process. This time, there was an immediate flash from the cockpit. The pilot's forehead struck the control panel and as the aircraft lurched to port, Arthur Kranz PhD, rolled towards the hatch and on towards the waves.

Crispin watched him die. Stark and silent. A few weeks ago, Crispin had craved this kind of action with all his might. Now, the only thought in his mind was escape. Reaching for Lucy, he dragged her past the open doorway and through the narrow corridor that led to the cockpit and the new and ghastly sight that awaited him there.

The second bolt from a flare gun was fixed in the pilot's scalp and still burning in his hair. Dragging the body to the floor, Crispin took his place by the controls. Moments later, a man's voice crackled on the radio and Crispin reached for the headset.

The reply was cold and clinical: "Tango Nine Zero, are you receiving me?"

In the last few minutes, the turbo prop had lost most of its altitude. Conscious that some sort of disaster was imminent, the air traffic control people remained calm. They asked him something impudent about *jeopardy*. Was he in jeopardy? *Yes.* On fire, with a dead man by the controls, a fantastic blonde a few inches to his left and a priceless global asset heading towards the sea.

"... your aircraft is losing altitude."

Which was true also, they *were* losing altitude and it seemed likely that the denser atmosphere was feeding the flames. It was time to take control and the aircraft was just waiting to respond. Neither engine showed signs of spluttering and Crispin impressed himself further by banking around and setting a new course for the English coast. Amidst a mass of alarms, lights and pre-digital dials, he even found an altimeter.

"Altitude five thousand feet and holding," he chanted, glancing up from the instrument panel and spying land. He saw a compass and convinced himself that he could take a reading. "Gimme a course for—"

But it was too late. He heard himself cough and guessed, correctly, that Lucy was coughing too. This aircraft wasn't going to make it back to Docklands City Airport or anywhere else. Besides, he had already noticed something else in the cockpit: a parachute. Reaching out to the wall, he freed one of them up and searched frantically for a second. None was to be found.

Given that he could barely fly anyway, ditching didn't sound that attractive either. A much better idea would be to reach the coast, hold her over 5,000 feet and bail out over dry land.

"Altitude?" he asked.

Crispin checked the altimeter again. In fact, their altitude was already below 5,000 feet and the inner arm on the pre-digital dial was spinning wildly.

"We're bailing out!"

There were three things he wanted to take with him: himself, the girl and something that might have been written by the Bard. Crispin stood up from the pilots seat and grabbed a pair of books from the floor. Then he reached out for Lucy, fumbling in his bid to tie them both together.

Further delays were likely to be deadly and Crispin paused, just short of the exit to stuff a foul smelling object in his mouth and a second one down his shirt. Everything else was going in the drink.

Time to jump. Having waited much longer than he really should have done, Crispin placed one hand on the ripcord and stepped forwards. The sound, the air and the lighting all changed in a single flash and the two of them jolted, fiercely on a tense harness. Lucy was a savage and untamed animal, digging her claws into her helpless victim, but she didn't break free and in a few more seconds, it occurred to Crispin that they might yet survive.

The wind was strong now and blowing inland and the beach beneath them a pale and sinuous strip that skirted the ocean and threatened to spoil his evening. In the event, he had little or no control over the landing anyway, and they hit the sand in a place where the breakers were white and receding and the ground beneath them soft.

She let him go. Crispin made it onto his knees. There was something very wet and very old between his teeth and he was ready to gag on it. Heavy with the sea, they heaved themselves inland until Crispin found the strength to reach a second document, trapped beneath his shirt. That one, at least was still unblemished and he threw the books westwards, lest he stumble in the water and soaked the pair of them. Glancing upwards he watched them fall onto dry sand.

"We still alive?" he heard her ask.

"Yes!"

And they were, but Crispin pinched himself anyway, just to be sure, because he was talking Lucy, and with Lucy, you never really knew either way.

Chapter 29

Even the greatest of institutions have an inception date and The British Museum is no different. The building first opened its doors to the public in 1759 and in its inaugural year, there were less than 5,000 guests. Today, that figure is closer to six million and the vast majority of these are overseas visitors. Amongst the chattering classes, much has been made of its steadfast commitment to free admission, but when one factors in the airfares, the hotel fees and the obligatory trips to the gift shop, it's hard to see the building as anything other than a massive cash cow for Britain.

Crispin, who had a reputation for poor time keeping, was able to get there early. Liaising via smart phone, the doctor and his cunning sidekick had agreed to meet outside the magnificent "Reading Rooms", where Karl Marx had once plotted the downfall of The Market. The boys weren't due on stage for at least half an hour and Roger had already expressed an interest in the Rosetta Stone. He didn't actually know what it was, but he knew it was famous and by the time they arrived, the entire edifice was already engulfed with school children.

Ploughing through a sea of blazers, Roger studied the plaque and grasped its significance with remarkable speed. Moments later, he described his plans to upgrade the Museum, his best one being a change to the dress code for the Security Guards. A couple of well-armed Spartans might do a lot to suppress some of these juvenile delinquents, and Crispin - who could see his point - asked Roger not to mention this in their forthcoming meeting.

"As a matter of fact," said Crispin, "I think we should go to that meeting, right *now*."

Now was the operative word and in the space of five minutes, they were received by a tall and terribly proper man in Harris Tweeds. Gesturing to a marble staircase, the man in Harris Tweeds took them down to the basement, a long stone corridor and so on to the prestigious oak panelled room that lay beyond. Here, the British Establishment had gathered in strength, all of them silent behind a broad white table cloth.

What – Crispin asked himself – were these people thinking?

He couldn't say. This type of client just didn't show up in your average outpatient clinic and he found them a difficult bunch to read. Closer to the door, he noticed a token woman in grey, fully equipped with a Government Issue note pad and a stub like pencil.

The chairman began by describing the physical condition of the books and the information within them. In that sense, things weren't quite as bad as they might have been. Prior to Arthur's arrival in Stratford, a number of pages had been photographed and, in his rush to reach the RSC lorry, Arthur had failed to destroy the relevant files. The ledgers for the Globe were entirely intact and in other circumstances, such a find might have been regarded as a miracle in itself. Sadly, these were not other circumstances and almost all of the prose documents had been lost. On a more positive note, the book that Crispin had stuffed down his shirt was worth a small fortune and had he come here in a different frame of mind, Crispin could have extracted a lot more from these idiots than they were about to give him.

"All of the books stolen by Doctor Kranz were lost, bar one intact volume, and a fifth, apparently unfinished work. Fifty per cent of material therein illegible. The committee notes further damage to a second volume by sand, salt water and…"

Removing his glasses for additional impact, the speaker did his best to sound severe.

"…*teeth* marks!"

Calm and collected in the face of it all, Crispin resisted the urge to cower. They were – he knew – only trying to downgrade the scale of his discovery.

"In summary, the board acknowledges the work of Doctor Shakespeare, not only for the original find but also for his bid to recover that same material in the aftermath of the theft. The aforementioned items will, therefore, be purchased at the standard rate."

The chairman reached over with what Crispin took to be a cheque and Roger made himself useful by standing up to receive it, asking, "That's pounds Sterling, is it?"

A strained silence fell down upon the boardroom.

"And who might you be?"

"I'm his financial advisor," said Roger, totally upbeat. "We almost brought one of those Hellenic digging types, but they thought I might be more useful."

And he was, checking the sales documents in mindless detail and making them all feel uncomfortable in the process. Then and only then, did Roger jot down the numbers and start to do maths. There was a second hiatus whilst he played with the calculator app and eventually called it good. The establishment seemed satisfied, the meeting ended and the boys escaped through the double doors and into the cold stone corridor from whence they had come.

It was over. Crispin moved to loosen his tie and Roger – who rarely apologised for anything – described a rare moment of self doubt.

"'Sorry I didn't make more of an impact in there. What sort of chance did we have against that lot? I mean, a 2-2 in Management and Economics!"

"Oh, I wouldn't worry about that, old man! That adds up to 4."

But Roger was back on his calculator again, working on something much more important.

"My best guess for the elimination of *all* Shakespearean debt has just been brought forward by twenty years."

This was good news indeed and Crispin was suddenly very attentive.

"It's a bit complicated," said Roger, "but basically, if you can hold down your current job, and don't go mad with the spending thing, you'll have no money whatsoever by Christmas."

Crispin asked for reassurance that his calculations were good. Had Roger included the bill for fixing the bullet holes in his speedboat?

Roger had.

"Actually, that was the first thing I listed."

Next, there was the issue of Crispin's mind boggling overdraft, the existing mortgage on his grade III listed cottage and the impending invoice from some obscure thatch maintenance group in Kenilworth. Had all of these figures being accounted for? They had and each and every one of them was waiting to be struck off the balance sheet, just as soon as the cheque came through. In any case, Roger told him, this wasn't a lottery win. It was a fee well deserved.

"These numskulls have really got egg in their face. You know, they actually invited Kranz over by fax? The FBI have found the paperwork. Sounds like the British Museum hasn't discovered e-mail yet. No one forced you to go down that sinkhole and you certainly didn't do it for the readies."

Then, without warning, the doors to the oak panelled room burst open and the Great and the Good came pouring out. First and foremost, came the stuffy faced chairman, curling his lip up as he walked on by. The rest of them were variations on a theme, most of them scowling the same, standard issue scowl until the man in Harris Tweeds arrived, picking up speed on his way to the Gents. Last but not least, came the unnamed lady in grey, her lips tightly sealed and her notebook firm against her waist.

It was time to get going. The boys progressed along the corridor and encountered that well-known staple of every British institution, a large, lumbering woman with a mop. Concerned that she might be causing an obstruction, the woman shuffled to one side and apologised for being there. Given that it was her job to keep the floor clean, this might be seen as a strange thing to come out with and for a second or two, Crispin wondered if there was some sort of message in her shuffling. Had his adventures made him important? Or do the cleaners of this world give way to every upright figure in a suit? He would never know.

A minute or so later, they were through the main exit and out onto sunlit steps.

"So, who was he?" asked Roger.

"Who was who?"

"*Shakespeare?* This bloke you're so mad on. What was he like? Was he a man?"

"Oh yes," said Crispin with real conviction. "He was a bona-fida Englishman. That's for sure."

"A man with a strong sex drive?"

By now, they had reached the forecourt and a party of Italian school girls were fast approaching. Roger was heading into unchartered territory and Crispin decided to divert to an empty patch of paving stones on their left. Relaxed in the shadow of a great institution, two slightly underweight young men resumed their conversation between the pillars.

"The sex thing," said Roger, as if he might have forgotten.

"Yes," said Crispin, trying to keep it all proper. "I should think he'd shag a house brick if it moved."

"How about motive? What did he write all these plays for?"

"For immediate performance."

"And the money? Did he ever think about money?"

"Oh yes," said Crispin. "He *always* thought about the money."

"How can you be so sure?"

"It's daft not to."

"And…" Something fresh and original had entered Roger's mind, "…do you think he'd be big in Hollywood? If he were around today?"

"Oh, for sure. He knew about sequels."

"You know what this sounds like, to me? This sounds like the opening chapter for a book."

"Yes," said Crispin, slightly more downbeat, "but I just made it all up."

"Well, I shouldn't let that worry you. That's what everybody else does."

They walked towards the main entrance and the pavement cafes across the road. Somewhere on the south side of Great Russell Street, there was a beautiful car with a chassis that had been carved from pure ash, and ninety seconds on the clock. Most of the people here had come to see the artefacts, but on this particular morning, the Morgan was stealing the show. Unable to contain his delight, Crispin reached for his keys and turned to say goodbye.

"It's not as popular as the Rosetta Stone, but it's certainly made its mark."

"Well, Doctor Shakespeare, if you ever find yourself further challenged by your expenses..."

"Next time," said Crispin, "I'll start by selling the Morgan."

They shook hands, one more time. Englishmen don't do tears or hugging, but Roger did make an effort to get the last word, shouting very loudly as the engine roared.

"You'll never sell that thing!"

Chapter 30

The summer was all but over and the long-awaited practice barbecue was finally upon them. A dozen or so local doctors had assembled in Jack's garden and the air was alight with the chatter of well-healed offspring and their equally well-healed wives.

As is the norm with these things, the day had progressed through several distinct phases. First, there is the one-off shopping trip to Ye Old English local megastore. Then, there is the emergence of the barbecue from the garden shed and the heaving of said barbecue across the lawn and towards a point of access. Limp meat hangs over blistering charcoal and the guests begin to arrive. And then, just as the bread buns come out, Crispin's disparate, ageing aunts appear en masse and rush to take control.

And no matter what happens next, this will always be England. Not one of these upper middle class revellers will ever surprise you, and no one will mention the elephant in the room. Because in the space of eight weeks, a previously unknown doctor from Stratford Upon Avon had risen to prominence on a global stage and in doing so, had given the world some – but limited – insight into a fabulous national icon.

It would appear that William Shakespeare had indeed lived and worked in this green and pleasant land and, to the gasping relief of the local tourist board, most of his childhood had been spent in the Midlands. Sadly, not one of the new documents made reference to his education and there was no more reason to suppose that Shakespeare attended Crispin's Grammar School now than there had been in the Spring.

With the diaries secure, Crispin had refused all contact with the press and focused instead on the job at hand. Conscious that he had never planned a barbecue before, he had summoned their dreary secretary into his consultation room and asked her to track down the Practice Diary from last year. Jack had long been a stickler for detail and Crispin knew that all of his transactions would be listed in that book. Ten minutes later, his secretary returned and Crispin told her to contact every tradesman with an invoice and ask them to deliver the exact same service again.

It worked. Crispin's barbecue was at least as good as the last one and in the opinion of many, the sauce had actually improved. And when every bread bun had been eaten and all the housework done, Crispin strolled towards Duncan, and decided to reveal his technique.

"Brilliant!" hissed Duncan, popping the cork on something red. "Brilliant! It *felt* like last year!"

And then Duncan poured the wine into two plastic beakers and suggested to Crispin that no matter how fantastic his summer had been, nothing had really changed in Stratford. But some things had. Over by the garden gate, the atmosphere was changing fast. Distant aunts had ceased to prattle and all eyes turned to a new and uninvited guest.

Crispin wasn't the only man to have suffered in August. Uncle Jack had taken his fair share of hits too and had spent most of this day resting in a battered wicker chair. Now at last, he had something to stand for, greeting her very politely with his one good hand.

Lucy smiled and Jack was smitten, leading her down to his much cherished rose bed where he claimed to have never employed any staff. And for her part, Lucy remained gracious, not even doing boredom whilst Jack revealed his favourite lawnmower. All in all, an astonishing performance, exceeded only by her recent statement to the police.

"Yeah, like the little dick was pushing me out of the hatch, with that gun on my butt."

Luckily, and as she explained in some detail, a small-time doctor from Stratford Upon Avon had grabbed Lucy with his bare hands, thus saving her from certain death.

Too bad about Kranz killing his own guys in error, but having said that, Kranz always had been a bit of a whacko with that pistol.

Watching from a safe distance, Crispin recalled the police reaction in his mind, "And is that how you remember it, Sir?"

It seemed unlikely that the officer's eyes had ever drifted from the aforementioned butt, but Crispin responded anyway.

"Sure, officer. Do you think a girl like this would lie to you?"

Back in the land of the living, Crispin wandered over to join Lucy and when Jack had returned to his chair, he heard her speak in a different voice.

"So, the old bastard got you! 'Took it all with him. You know, he's probably up there now, churning through every page in his own little cloud."

Crispin did his best to sound defiant. Material had been lost, sure, but there were two good books in the museum and in the course of time, their contents would be common knowledge.

"Weren't they all wet?"

"Yes," said Crispin, "but you can just about read them."

She asked if he would be allowed to keep one. Crispin said that he wouldn't and the American remained courteous, even stretching her hand as far as *sympathy*.

"Wouldn't you have liked to have had a book that gave you all the intel on the big guy?"

"Not really." he told her. "Besides, I already have one."

And then Crispin held out one hand, afraid – perhaps – that she might refuse to take it. He needn't have worried. Lucy was a natural performer and she hadn't come here to let him down. On the edge of the rose bed, she responded in kind and Crispin led her back to the stables and a much loved pony, wondering, as he did so, if her name was really Lucy at all.